DRIFTWOOD LADY

Brogan McNally did not imagine that he would be wanted as an outlaw when he found himself in Driftwood. When Betty Crossland suggested that he murder her brothers, McNally refused. However, he later discovers that her father and two of her three brothers have been murdered and he is the accused. McNally's only chance of proving his innocence lies with the surviving brother, Jonathan Crossland, who escaped to Sulphur Springs . . . With a US marshal trailing him, can McNally prove his innocence?

L. D. TETLOW

DRIFTWOOD LADY

Complete and Unabridged

LINFORD
Leicester

First published in Great Britain in 2005 by
Robert Hale Limited
London

First Linford Edition
published 2006
by arrangement with
Robert Hale Limited
London

British Library CIP Data

Tetlow, L. D.
  Driftwood lady.—Large print ed.—
Linford western library
  1. Western stories 2. Large type books
  I. Title
  823.9'14 [F]

  ISBN 1–84617–245–4

Published by
F. A. Thorpe (Publishing)
Anstey, Leicestershire

Set by Words & Graphics Ltd.
Anstey, Leicestershire
Printed and bound in Great Britain by
T. J. International Ltd., Padstow, Cornwall

This book is printed on acid-free paper

1

Brogan McNally, saddle tramp and proud of it, had a distinctly uneasy feeling as he rode slowly down the main street of the one-time fairly large but now small, one-street town of Drift-wood. Apart from one house apparently still occupied, where the side streets had been there was now nothing but piles of rotting timbers. If it was not so much the dilapidated state of the town which exuded a slight air of menace, it was most certainly the three youths, each carrying a rifle and a-sneering at him from the boardwalk outside what appeared to be an empty building. In fact there seemed to be more buildings empty than occupied even in the main street. The whole town had an aura of decay. Brogan had passed through many Driftwoods during his years of travelling.

In themselves and the normal way such youths would have presented no problems to Brogan and he would simply have ignored them. More often than not youths and even some adults would pick on him for no other reason than that he was what he was — a saddle tramp. As such, he was apparently fair game to many gunhappy youths and men.

His kind, along with Indians and Negroes, were generally despised and very often, he had to concede, not without good reason. Brogan McNally, however, prided himself on being very different from the normal run of saddle tramps and drifters. Most would steal almost anything at any opportunity and, whenever possible, rob and even murder a man — or a woman — for little more than the odd coins in their pockets. Not so Brogan McNally. It was his proud boast that *'I ain't never murdered nobody an' I ain't never stole nothin' off nobody'*. This was actually quite true — he was not a killer or a thief, he paid his way whenever possible or went without. He had, though, killed many times, but always in self-defence or with good justification — at least according to him.

His biggest failing was that he could not help but somehow become involved in other peoples' business. In other words he was just plain nosy. His other big failing was that he was a sucker for a hard-luck story and always found himself siding with the apparent under-dog. It was not always a case of *not* minding his own business or listening to someone else's woes that got him into trouble. He also had the unfortu-nate knack of attracting it, very often for no apparent reason other than he was plainly a saddle tramp.

When it came to situations such as the one he believed was about to present itself, he always tried to avoid trouble. In fact he tried to avoid any form of confrontation wherever and whenever possible. At least that was always what he told himself. The reality was often quite different and trouble always seemed to find a way of finding him.

Usually, when they could get little or no reaction from him, most grew bored with taunting him and moved away. On this occasion, however, he had noticed that without exception, the few residents of Driftwood who were about had gone out of their way to avoid the youths. This indicated to him that they were plainly known troublemakers or that they too had drifted into town and were making their presence felt. He had no way of knowing into which category they fell and he was not really interested. In the past he had come across outlaws ranging in age from fifteen to well over fifty. In most towns the youths would be the problem of the local sheriff but in this case it seemed that Driftwood was now too small to support a full-time lawman.

That apparent lack of a sheriff was, in most cases, something of a bonus as far as Brogan was concerned. They were, as often as not, the first to attempt to move him on or even threaten him and one thing he disliked more than anything else was being told when to leave anywhere. He always left eventually, but always in his own time, which was very often quicker than when ordered to leave.

That these three were little more than youths seemed more than obvious. He doubted if any one of them was over eighteen years old and the youngest appeared to be no more than fifteen or sixteen years of age. However, years of experience had taught him that young men such as these, young bucks out to prove themselves and who plainly fancied their chances with a gun, were often far more dangerous than most seasoned gunfighters.

Most had the unfortunate habit of shooting rather than talking, which was usually because their vocabulary and reasoning were very limited. Because of this, it appeared that their one aim in life was to prove to everyone that *they* were without fear, that *they* were the fastest and most accurate with a gun there ever was, but most of all they needed people to be afraid of them. To them, fear meant power. Brogan, although always cautious, was certainly not afraid. Despite their youth, Brogan knew that should it become necessary, he would have no hesitation and probably no problem in killing all three of them.

He did not enjoy killing anyone but on the other hand it certainly did not bother him. During his many years of drifting he had sent his fair share of such people to their grave. As far as he was concerned if any such action was necessary then he would have no hesitation in taking it. He had the feeling that in this case it just might become necessary. The youths were plainly looking for somebody on whom they could show just how good and brave they were.

He pulled up outside what appeared to be a saloon-cum-general store, the only such establishment of either kind in Driftwood, and dismounted. He noted that the youths had left their position outside the adjoining building and were now sneering at him again as they slowly and arrogantly walked the short boardwalk. The thumbs of their free hands were tucked into the tops of their trousers or into their belts and for the first time Brogan saw that though they carried handguns they did not possess proper gunbelts.

Two of them, the two older youths, had their guns pushed through their belts whilst the youngest had what seemed to be a home-made shoulder holster. He was now even more convinced that they were fully intent on trouble. It was very rare for young men to carry guns at all, except possibly scatterguns when around the farm, and most certainly very rare to be so heavily armed.

He led his horse to a water-trough at the side of the store, left her untethered safe in the knowledge that she would not wander off no matter what happened, scooped up some water for himself, swirled it round in his mouth and then spat it out before turning to face the youths. By that time they had positioned themselves outside the door of the saloon-cum-store.

There were two reasons as to why Brogan had ventured into Driftwood; the first was that his horse had cast a shoe less than half an hour before he had known the town even existed, and the second was that he needed a few supplies, mainly salt, beans, sugar and coffee and flour.

He was more than capable of living off the land even in the most inhospitable of deserts. He had done so for many years, more years than he cared to count and had in that time eaten many strange things, including beetles, grubs and bugs. He always claimed and was as often as not right, that there was food everywhere if you only knew where to look and were not too particular about what you ate. Even if he went without sugar, coffee, flour and beans, salt in a form he could use was almost impossible to find and vital to good health and survival.

He was a little surprised when the youths stood to one side to allow him to enter the store but he was very alert to the fact that they crowded in behind him. The look on the store-owner's face told him that he had good reason to be alert.

The place was much as he had expected and had seen in many other small towns, consisting of a small bar and four tables with chairs to his right whilst the remainder of the space to his left was given over to all the things a general store might sell. He looked about for a few moments, sniffed the rather musty air and ordered a glass of beer.

'Make that three more, Jed,' one of the youths ordered. 'Our friend here is payin'.'

Brogan turned and looked about the room in an exaggerated fashion.

'You got friends?' he said to the youths. 'I don't see none. Anyhow, are you sure you're old enough to drink strong liquor? I'd say you've only just been weaned off your ma's tit-milk.'

'You just watch your mouth, old man,' snapped the eldest of the three. 'I said for you to buy us a drink. You deaf or somethin'?'

Brogan quite deliberately stuck a finger in his ear and wiggled it about before removing it and looking closely at the tip of the finger as though it had something slightly offensive on it.

'What's that you say, *boy*?' he asked. 'You'll have to excuse an old man like me. Deafness is somethin' what happens to all of us as we get older. You should ask your pa about that, if you know who your pa is, that is.'

Brogan was far from deaf. He maintained that he could hear a fly land on a piece of dung a hundred yards away. That was plainly an exaggeration, but his hearing was indeed very acute, and his reactions were very swift. Not

10

only that, he was an excellent shot and very fast with it.

'OK, old man,' said the youth with what he thought was a knowing grin. 'You had your fun. Now do like I say an' buy us a drink each. You're a stranger round here so I guess we got to make allowances for you not knowin' the rules. The rule is folk in this town do whatever we tell 'em to do an' part of that is that we never pay for our drinks. In fact we never pay for nothin', nothin' at all. Do I make myself clear?'

Once again Brogan pretended to clean out his ear.

'If you never pay then I guess you don't drink that much,' he said. 'But then maybe milk is cheap in these parts. I also have rules an' one of them is that I never buy drinks for nobody, especially not strong liquor for children. I don't approve of minors drinkin' alcohol.'

He deliberately chose the words *children* and *minors* knowing that they would be far more offensive than any

11

other words or phrases. He smiled to himself; he had very quickly slipped into his old habit of taunting people, thereby making his own situation worse. That, unfortunately, was a side of his nature over which he appeared to have little control.

His taunting appeared to be working; the eldest youth and the only one to speak thus far, suddenly snarled and marched up to Brogan. He was only about two feet away when he suddenly, and foolishly, attempted to push the barrel of his rifle into Brogan's neck.

Brogan, however, had been expecting just such a thing. In fact he had sensed rather than seen the slight change in the way the youth held his rifle. Brogan's Colt was suddenly jammed underneath the youth's chin forcing his head backwards. The youth gasped slightly, stared wide-eyed and terrified at him and seemed to have difficulty breathing.

'You were sayin', son?' prompted Brogan. 'Somethin' about me buyin' you a drink, wasn't it? Just think on this, boy. If I should squeeze this trigger right now your brains — if you have any that is — are goin' to end up splattered all over the roof. You won't be interested in who buys the drinks after that, will you.' He spoke to the other two. 'Drop your guns, all of 'em. I don't want no trouble, all I want is somebody to shoe my horse an' for the storekeeper to sell me some supplies. After that I'll be on my way.'

'Best do as he says, boys,' a voice boomed from the doorway. Brogan had seen the man enter the room and had been prepared for anything he might do. 'I'd say he's more'n capable of blowin' your head off, Jamie,' continued the man. 'And don't you two go thinkin' you could get the better of him either. He'd probably kill you before you had time to react an' still have time to spare to wipe his ass between shots if he wanted to.'

'You know these scum?' asked Brogan.

'I ought to,' replied the man with a dry laugh. 'My wife gave birth to 'em an' she assures me I'm their father. Like most men though, I've only got her word on that but they call me *Pa*.' By that time all three youths had dropped their guns. 'I'm Sam Crossland, I own most of everythin' in these parts worth ownin'. The boy you got stuck to the end of your gun is my eldest, Jamie. The other two are Nathan an' Jonathan.'

'You should teach them to respect their elders,' grunted Brogan as he relaxed and lowered his gun. 'I reckon a good bare-assed beltin' would do 'em a power of good even as old as they are.'

'Could be you're right,' sighed Sam Crossland. 'Their ma spoils 'em though. She won't have no beatin' of 'em, never has done, spoils 'em rotten she does. They can never do no harm in her eyes. OK, boys, pick up your guns an' get yourselves back home. I don't think you realize just how close you all came to gettin' yourselves killed.'

'We could've dealt with him, Pa,' muttered the second son, Nathan. 'He's nought but a dirty old saddle bum an' there ain't nobody what gives a darn what happens to no saddle bum.'

'You could be right at that,' conceded Sam Crossland. 'About his bein' a dirty old saddle bum. You is very wrong about bein' able to deal with him though, he looks like a professional to me. Saddle tramp he may be. Yeah, I'd say the boy was right about nobody givin' a damn, Mr . . . er . . . Wouldn't you?'

'Not quite,' said Brogan. 'I for one would care, but I don't suppose anybody else would. The name's McNally, Brogan McNally. My friends, what few I might have, call me Brogan, but your boys can call me Mr McNally. It ain't fittin' for minors to call their elders by given names.'

'Then I'll call you McNally too,' said Crossland. 'Not *Mr* McNally, just McNally. I wouldn't want to be seen takin' sides against my own kin now, would I? Go on, boys, get the hell out of here while you still can.'

The youths muttered under their breath, picked up their guns and stomped out of the store. Brogan picked up his glass of beer, downed it in one gulp and ordered another.

'Fine drop of beer,' he admitted. 'Nice taste an' cool, just how I like it.'

'I'll have one too, Jed,' said Crossland. 'Yeah, Jed here brews an' keeps the finest beer for hundreds of miles around.' He looked Brogan up and down for a short while. 'Saddle bum you might be,' he said eventually. 'But I've seen many gunfighters in my time — used to be one myself as a matter of fact — an' I'd say you was a man who knew exactly how to handle himself and a gun. I knew it as soon as I clapped eyes on you. I'd say you could be a very dangerous man, McNally, very dangerous. I'd hate to get on the wrong side of you.'

'Don't know about that,' said Brogan. 'I might be dangerous to somebody who tries to kill me but I like to mind my own business an' keep away from trouble whenever I can. You is quite wrong about one thing though, I ain't no gunfighter, never have been.'

'Words!' laughed Crossland. 'All words. OK, so you ain't no regular gunfighter. You probably don't hire yourself out but I'm not wrong in sayin' that you sure know how to handle one.'

'Maybe that's somethin' you should teach them boys of yours,' said Brogan. 'How to recognize somebody who is better than they could ever be. Chances are they'll never see twenty years if they carry on like that.'

'Thanks for the advice,' said Crossland. 'I'll work on it. Their trouble is they don't come up against folk like you that often. Most saddle bums do as they're told or make a run for it. I think Jamie's killed a couple of 'em, but he won't admit to it an' I can't be sure. Not that it matters anyhow.'

'There's always the exception,' said Brogan. 'The saddle bum who ain't scared an' who doesn't run an' who can handle a gun.'

'Just so,' agreed Crossland. 'That's what I tried tellin' 'em just now. OK, Jed, thanks for the beer.' Brogan had noted that he had not paid for it. 'I'll be gettin' back. I just came in to tell you I got me a consignment of salt beef comin' in next week, best quality too. I'm sure you wouldn't want to miss out on the chance of buyin' some at a fair price. Goodbye, McNally,' he said to Brogan. 'I hope we don't meet again.'

He raised his hat slightly and left the store. Brogan watched his departure through the grimy window before turning to Jed, the owner of the store.

'Salt beef!' sighed Jed. 'Always it's salt beef. I got me enough salt beef to start my own business sellin' it.'

'So don't buy no more,' suggested Brogan.

'So don't buy no more!' replied Jed with a derisive laugh. 'Man, it's plain to see you're a stranger in these parts, Mr McNally. When Sam Crossland suggests anythin' you act on it even if it does mean buyin' more of his damned salt beef. Folk round here just don't want no salt beef.'

'I didn't see him pay for his beer either,' said Brogan. 'He seems to have taught his sons that much at least.'

'The Crosslands never pay for nothin',' muttered Jed.

'It can't be much of a livin' for you out here,' said Brogan. 'Seems to me the town's half empty.'

'Oh, don't be fooled by its looks,' said Jed. 'It's quiet now durin' the week but come Friday night, Saturday an' Sunday the old place gets quite busy. Even the old church is open on Sunday mornin'. We ain't got no regular minister no more but we got what they call a lay preacher. There's plenty of places for folk to bed down for a night or two, as you've probably noticed. It's nothin' like it used to be when there was gold up in the hills, but it's enough to keep me goin'. Mostly they is farmers but there's still a few prospectors about.'

'And how does Sam Crossland fit

into the picture?' Brogan asked. 'Didn't he say somethin' about ownin' most things?'

'He owns a ranch, only ranch in these parts,' explained Jed. 'Well, I suppose it is a ranch of sorts. He runs about a thousand head of cattle, upwards of three thousand or more sheep and breeds horses. He sells all of them to the army out at Fort Leveson and Fort Kenyon. Fort Leveson is about thirty miles east and Fort Kenyon about forty miles west. He buys in things like salt beef for the army as well. Only trouble is he insists on me buyin' some every time he gets a shipment. He's got most of the farmers round here tied to him as well. He has the contract with the army for supplyin' all meat, flour, vegetables and fruit. Apart from me buyin' a bit off 'em, if a farmer wants to sell his produce, he has to deal through Crossland. He dictates the price and there's not much anyone can do about it.'

'It must be a nice little business,' said

Brogan. 'What was that he said about bein' a gunfighter himself?'

'Only thing I know is rumour,' said Jed. 'They say he was a hired gunfighter in his younger days and that he got most of his money by stealing a gold shipment he was supposed to be guarding. Apparently nobody could ever prove he had anything to do with it though. They also say he got the contract for his meat and horses because he had a hold over some army general or other. However he did it, he sure built himself a nice business.'

'All of which makes it rather surprisin' that his sons act the way they do,' said Brogan. 'They must have a very easy life and want for nothin' yet they seem to want to spoil it all. Perhaps they have it too easy. They could be plain bored.'

'They're just plain bad,' said Jed. 'Born bad and bred bad. They won't do any cattle herdin' or anythin' like that, too much like hard work. Crossland's wife worked in a whorehouse in

Phoenix even after they married. Then she got pregnant and he bought up out here. Neither of them ever had any control over them boys an' never will. One day somebody's goin' to snap and do for those boys an' it'll be their own fault. He has a daughter, she's the eldest an' the only one with any sense at all. She's completely different from her brothers. She ought to be the one to take over the business, not any of the boys. Jamie thinks it's all goin' to him an' he's probably right about that. Him bein' the eldest boy an' all that.'

'Well,' said Brogan. 'It ain't none of my business. Is there anywhere I can get my horse seen to? She cast a shoe not long ago this mornin'.'

'Luke Briscoe is the only one these days,' said Jed. 'There was a time when there were three blacksmiths and farriers in town but them days have long gone. Luke isn't a blacksmith but he's a good farrier and there's just about enough work to keep him occupied, even if Crossland does expect his own horses seein' to for nothin'. I think he pays for the ones he sells to the army though, too many to expect him not to. God only knows how we'll manage when Luke finally hangs up his tools, he ain't got nobody to take it on after him.'

'Where can I find this Luke?' asked Brogan.

'End of the street,' said Jed. 'Can't miss it, he's usually there.'

'Thanks,' said Brogan. 'I'll take her along now. While I'm away you can put me up two pound of coffee, two pound of sugar, two pound of flour, four pound of beans an' a pound of salt — oh, and I'll take some of that salt beef off your hands. I'll be back.'

'Coffee beans or ground coffee?' asked Jed. 'They've started doin' proper ground-up coffee now. It's a bit dearer but it's a hell of lot more convenient.'

'Beans,' said Brogan. 'I've been usin' coffee beans all my life. I'm too old to change my ways now. Anyhow I don't trust these newfangled ideas, you never know how much is the real thing an' how much is sweepin's an' dirt off the floor. 'Sides it gives me somethin' to do, grindin' 'em up, that is.'

Brogan led his horse along the street and found Luke Briscoe, the farrier, in the process of shoeing a large work-horse. He waited for him to finish before showing Luke his horse.

'Cast it this mornin',' explained Brogan. 'How much for a new one?'

'Two dollars,' said Luke. 'One dollar for the shoe, one dollar for my labour.' He lifted the horse's other hoofs and studied them. 'It'll only be a matter of days or even hours before she loses these others as well,' he continued. 'I'll do all four for six dollars. One dollar for each shoe an' two dollars for my labour.'

'That sounds fair enough,' agreed Brogan, handing Luke a ten-dollar bill.

The farrier scrabbled around in a tin and eventually found four dollars in change. At that moment a black-haired woman on a horse drew up. Unusually she was wearing trousers. She looked down at Brogan for a few seconds before nodding briefly. She dismounted and tied her horse to a rail.

'Take a look at his front right, Luke,' she said. 'He seems to be limping a bit. I noticed it two days ago but I think it's getting worse.'

'Sure thing, Miss Betty,' said Luke. He went to pick up the horse's hoof.

'No hurry,' she said. 'I've got a couple of things to see to. Deal with Mr McNally's horse first. I'm sure his need is greater than mine.'

'You know my name,' said Brogan.

'By now everybody in the county will know exactly who you are and what you did to my brothers.' She laughed, plainly finding it highly amusing. 'My brothers they might be but it's about time somebody put them in their place. I'll be back in about an hour, Luke.'

'She looks like a dangerous woman,' observed Brogan as he watched her walk away swinging her hips. It was obvious that she knew he was watching her.

'I'd feel safer with her brothers,' said Luke. 'At least you usually know what mountain lions, wolves an' scorpions are goin' to do. I think she could outrattle a rattlesnake.'

'I know just what you mean,' said Brogan. 'Just like a mother bear with cubs, you never know what they'll do.'

2

The farrier picked up the hoof of Brogan's horse and started to clean it. Suddenly he stopped and slowly eased out a sharp stone. As he did so some pus oozed out. He called Brogan over and showed him.

'Infected,' pronounced the farrier. 'I can't shoe her in this state. It ain't too bad but it needs a couple of days at least. I can treat it if you like. I'm the nearest thing this county has to an animal doctor, or a people doctor come to that. I know most things about cows and horses. They also reckon I'm pretty good at fixin' broken bones, pullin' teeth an' stitchin' folk up.'

'Damn!' muttered Brogan. 'Are you sure there's nothin' you can do straightaway? I don't particularly want to hang about Driftwood.'

'Choice is yours, Mr McNally,' said

Luke. 'Try to force her now an' it will only make things worse. I've got a special tincture that'll soon clear it up but it'll take a couple of days, three at the most. It's an old Indian remedy but it sure seems to work on horses an' people. Leastways I ain't never had no complaints from either people or horses.'

'There ain't nothin' wrong with good Indian remedies,' said Brogan. 'I reckon they've saved my life a couple of times.'

'Some folk find it hard to accept that any Indian might know somethin' they don't,' said Luke. 'Thing is, it really does need a couple of days at least, make her go on now an' you'll only make it worse. You'll probably end up havin' to shoot her an' I can guarantee you'll be out in some desert or somethin'. That's usually the way these things happen.'

'I guess that explains why she was limpin',' said Brogan. 'I thought it was just because of a loose shoe. OK, old girl,' he said to the horse as he stroked her muzzle, 'I guess like usual we ain't got nowheres in particular to go or any particular time to be there. Go ahead, fix her up,' he said to the farrier. 'Me an' her've been together a long time now, we understand each other. I'd hate for anythin' to happen to her now just 'cos I didn't want to hang about somewheres.'

'Treatment, new shoes, feed an' stablin',' said Luke thoughtfully. 'OK, ten dollars will cover everythin'.'

'Ten dollars!' muttered Brogan. 'OK, I guess so. Does that include me beddin' down alongside her?'

'I suppose so,' agreed Luke. 'You don't have to bed down here though. We ain't got no hotel, whorehouse or roomin' house no more, but there's no shortage of empty places.'

'I'd prefer bein' with my horse,' said Brogan. 'She stinks an' I stink but at least we're used to each other. I guess my saddle will be all right here.'

'Couldn't be safer,' said Luke. 'You can leave anythin' you want, includin' your guns if you want to. Last time anybody stole anythin' in this county was over two years ago. He was a drifter, much like yourself, who stole a blueberry-pie off Widder Graham.' He laughed. 'Strange woman was Widder Graham. She followed him an' emptied two scattergun cartridges into his balls. Mind you, most folk said that that was not because he stole the pie — an' they was probably right — but because he preferred her cookin' to her body. Can't say as I blame him for that though, Widder Graham was just about the biggest woman you ever did see in your life. Her cookin' warn't up to much either, everybody knew that. Apparently she didn't kill him, but I reckon she might as well have done. I've heard of circumcision but that sure was a bit extreme. Never did find out what happened to him after that.'

'The Crosslands seem to take whatever they want and not pay,' said Brogan. 'That's stealin'.'

'That ain't quite the same,' said

Luke. 'OK, so maybe they do take what they want, but on the other hand they provide quite a few jobs an' the farmers have a guaranteed market for their crops. Most folk are prepared to put up with a few things 'cos of that. Biggest problem is them boys of his but there ain't nobody ready to take 'em on, on account of who their pa is. I know he thinks they're a waste of time but then again he won't just stand by while folk take it into their own hands to do somethin' about them.'

'He didn't do much just now when I tackled the eldest, Jamie,' said Brogan. 'Maybe you haven't heard about that, though. It's only just happened. It seems he even found it a bit amusin'.'

'I heard somethin',' said Luke. 'Bad news travels round this town, almost before it's happened sometimes. Thing is, you didn't actually do anythin' to him, did you? I mean you didn't kill or shoot at any of them, you just scared 'em all a bit. Anyhow, I think Sam Crossland was really quite pleased somebody stood up for themselves against them. He reckons it teaches them how to look after themselves. He'd soon object if folk started makin' a habit of it though. You're a stranger, you'll soon be gone, the likes of me have to live here. We have to be more careful.'

'I suppose so,' said Brogan. 'I'm hungry but it seems there's nowhere to buy a hot meal. I don't suppose there's anywhere where I can get some hot food? Maybe some farmhouse or somethin'.'

'The only way you'll get any hot food is if you cook it yourself,' said Luke. 'Widder Graham ain't even around no more. She'd always cook a man a mess of a meal an' there was only ever one charge for it. She passed away a couple of months ago. Food poisonin' they say.' Somehow, Brogan was rather grateful for that fact.

At the store, Jed agreed to hold Brogan's purchases until he was ready. For his dinner, Brogan bought a large slice of smoked ham, two eggs and a large turnip complete with green top. This was a feast as far as he was concerned, even if he did have to cook it himself. He also bought himself two cheroots. He was not a regular smoker but he did enjoy one occasionally. He was about to leave when Betty Crossland came in. She smiled knowingly and almost invitingly, or so he thought.

'I heard about your horse,' she said. 'Personally I'd shoot it. It must be almost as old as you are and it looks about ready to drop dead. I can sell you a decent horse.'

'I can think of plenty of *people* in a worse state than she is,' said Brogan. 'Folk don't go round shootin' people just on account of they is a bit old, do they? Let's just say she's an old friend an' I don't go round shootin' my friends. Anyhow, even if I could afford the askin' price for another horse, which I can't, it'd mean me havin' to get used to another one an' it used to me. Me an' her know each other pretty well now. We talk all the time even if she does usually disagree with most things I do or say. I have to admit though, that she's usually right.'

'You've been drifting too long,' Betty Crossland said, laughing. 'All that sun has addled your brain.'

'At least I got a brain to addle,' said Brogan. 'That's more'n can be said for them brothers of yours.'

'I'll say *amen* to that, Mr McNally,' she said with a loud laugh.

Brogan returned to Luke Briscoe's forge where he used the hearth to cook his food and an hour later he was enjoying a rather burned ham, scrambled eggs, turnip and turnip greens. He had just finished when he became aware that he was being watched. He looked up to see Betty Crossland again.

'Can I help you, ma'am?' he asked.

'No,' she replied. 'I just came in to pay Luke and saw you.'

'You looked like you was thinkin',' said Brogan. 'Now I'm as red-blooded as the next man but I can't believe that you was lookin' at me with thoughts about my body. They tell me I smell pretty bad but I can't say as I ever noticed. Anyhow, I'm probably older'n your pa.'

'As a matter of fact I *was* thinking about you,' she said. 'Not in that way though. There's not many men about these parts worth a second look and the few who are, are married. I most certainly am not desperate enough for a man to think about you or anyone else in that way. In fact the very thought of that filthy body of yours on top of mine makes me feel sick. I'm just curious, that's all.'

'I guess that tells me where I stand,' said Brogan. 'Most women seem to think the same and the few what do take to me usually try to insist on me havin' a bath with real soap. Hot water, soap an' me just don't agree, no sir. So, you is curious about me? What the hell is there about me to be curious about? I'm a nobody, a drifter or, as your brother Nathan put it, a stinkin' old saddle bum. I'm not the best-lookin' man in the world an' I don't have any money. So what is there to be curious about?'

'You're right,' she said. 'You are a stinking, no-good saddle bum, but I'm still curious. Stinking and a no-good you might be, but it seems you are not easily scared off and can handle yourself.' She turned and took the reins of her horse. 'Yeah,' she said looking at him again. 'I wonder . . . ' She did not finish her sentence as she laughed and mounted the animal. She was soon lost to sight. Brogan remained thoughtful for some time.

'A dangerous woman,' Brogan muttered to himself eventually. 'I don't know quite what it is about her, but I'd say she was one woman best avoided.'

The remainder of that day and that night passed quietly enough. In the evening Brogan treated himself to a couple of beers and another cheroot. There were only three other people in the saloon and they studiously ignored him. He gathered that he was the main topic of conversation judging by their whispers and the constant, furtive looks in his direction.

It was obviously very rare for anyone to take on and get the better of any of the Crosslands. He had the feeling that wagers were being laid and taken as to how long he would last. He did not mind them not talking to him, in fact he usually preferred his own company.

The following morning, as was his normal habit, he was awake and about just as dawn broke. Luke Briscoe arrived about an hour later, examined the injured hoof of Brogan's horse and applied some more of his tincture.

'Gettin' better already,' he said. 'She might be ready tomorrow sometimes but I'd give it another day if I was you. The longer you can leave it the better. You ain't in no hurry to get anywhere are you?'

'Where's there to get to?' asked Brogan.

'Apart from Fort Leveson or Fort

Kenyon, there's Sulphur Springs. That's about five days' ridin' due north. Big town, lots of saloons, gamin' houses an' whorehouses, if you like that kind of thing. They tell me some folk actually pay to bathe in the pools of natural hot water there. Reckon they're good for the body. Hot water comes out of the ground an' some people reckon it's good for their health. They're mostly women but then women are like that sometimes, full of weird ideas. In some places the hot water gushes out in big fountains sometimes reachin' twenty or thirty feet high. I seen it a couple of times but it sure does stink. They reckon that's the smell of the sulphur, whatever that is.'

'Sounds like a good place to avoid,' said Brogan. 'Me an' hot water don't see eye to eye at the best of times. Never have done, never will. I had me a couple of baths against my will an' both gave me one hell of a cold.'

'I figured that much,' said Luke. 'Most saddle bums are the same though. I suppose you get out of the habit of washin' or bathin'.'

'Some of us never had the habit in the first place,' said Brogan. 'I don't ever remember my ma washin' me when I was a small child. Only thing she ever did for me was teach me to read an' write an' I thank her for that. I never knew who my pa was an' neither did she.'

'Well, as long as your horse can live with it, I guess I can,' said Luke with a laugh. 'That foot of hers ain't as bad as I thought it was but she still needs a bit of rest to make sure.'

'I'm glad to hear it,' said Brogan. 'The sooner the better as far as I'm concerned. By the way, that Betty Crossland was by here last night, lookin' to pay you, or so she said — '

'One thing abut Miss Betty,' interrupted Luke, 'is she ain't one for expectin' somethin' for nothin'. She allus pays her way. Only wish she could get her pa an' her brothers to do the same.'

'Yeah, somethin' tells me she'd be like that,' said Brogan. 'But like we said yesterday, there's somethin' about her what just don't sit right with me. It was the same last night. Normally I don't think twice about anybody, 'specially a woman, but she . . . Well, she just ain't right.'

'Are you scared of her?' asked Luke, apparently quite serious. 'I know I am an' I know most folk round here are. Most are scared of her brothers too, but not in the same way as they are of her. There's some who reckon that if you shot her she'd get right back on her feet or the bullet would pass straight through an' do her no harm at all. It's even said that she's what they call a witch. Why folk should think like that about her I don't know. She's always been very fair with me an' everybody else as far as I know. She always pays her debts.'

'Scared, no,' said Brogan. 'I'm just very wary about her, that's all. As for bein' a witch, no, she's just as human as you or me. It's just her mind what's different. It's nothin' more than a case of what she thinks an' how she thinks.' He thought for a moment. 'That's it! She thinks things out an' is all the more dangerous for it. She uses folk without them realizin'. Why do I get the feelin' that she's workin' on me for some reason? More important, why *should* she be workin' on me?'

A short time later Brogan also asked Jed, the storeowner, his opinion of Betty Crossland. He said much the same as Luke Briscoe had but he put the aura and mystique that had apparently built up around her down to nothing more than the fact that she was who she was — a Crossland. Brogan was not quite so certain.

There was a river a short distance out of town. It was not particularly wide or deep but there were plenty of trees along its banks. The beauty of nature was hardly something in which Brogan was all that interested. He knew what type of country he liked best and the time of year he liked best in certain areas. His interest in things which grew or moved was primarily confined as to whether or not they were edible. He had never been one to admire the scenery for its own sake. He just knew he preferred the wide open spaces to the overpowering closeness of the town.

Having little else to do, he found himself sitting on the river-bank. It was one of those occasions when his mind was more or less completely blank. His eyes saw things but his mind did not. In fact, his mind was so blank that his usually very receptive senses did not hear her.

Normally he would have heard even the faintest of footsteps, the snap of a small twig or even the faint scuff of leather on the ground. This was one of the very few occasions when he heard nothing. Later, he even briefly thought of her reputation for being a witch and gave serious thought to her having the power to move without sound. Briefly, only very briefly.

'Good afternoon, Mr McNally,' she said. Brogan spun round, his hand on his gun. 'I never had you down as a nature-lover,' she continued. It was almost as though she had read his mind. 'I come here myself sometimes, when I have things to think about. It's very relaxing.'

'Afternoon, Miss Betty,' said Brogan, releasing the grip on his gun. 'I hope you don't mind me callin' you that?'

'Not at all, Mr McNally' she said smiling disarmingly. 'Everybody else does. How much longer do you expect to be here in Driftwood?'

'Should be on my way in a couple of days at most,' said Brogan. 'Luke reckons my horse should be all right by then. I sure hope so, I hate bein' forced to stay anywhere, 'specially a place like Driftwood. I've seen a few places what've seen better days but Driftwood is about the worse. A real ghost town.'

'Originally built on gold,' she said. 'That was before my time of course but there are still one or two who remember those days. There's even a couple of prospectors still working the hills. They still find some gold I hear. Yes, Driftwood is indeed a ghost town. I would have thought a place like this would have suited you better than a large, busy town. Correct me if I'm wrong, but I get the impression that you prefer your own company, that you are a loner. I would have thought the wide open spaces were more to your liking.'

'You are a very observant woman,' said Brogan. 'Yes, ma'am, there's nothin' I like better than the open spaces. Open spaces an' nobody but me an' my old horse for company.'

'My father tells me that you were very fast with that gun of yours,' she said, casually. 'My brother Jamie always says that he is the fastest man with a gun round here but Father says you left him for cold.'

'It ain't always the man who is fastest on the draw who wins,' said Brogan. 'In any straight draw there's probably a whole heap of men faster'n me. What gives the likes of me the edge is knowin' the signs, knowin' what a man is goin' to do an' actin' before he can. That brother of yours sent out so many signals even a blind man could've seen 'em. Anyhow, I'm sure you really couldn't care less how good I am with a gun. Only thing is, right now you is sendin' out a hell of a lot of signals but I have to admit I just don't know how to read 'em. They must mean somethin'.'

'You are not quite correct about me not being interested in your shooting prowess, Mr McNally,' she said. 'Perhaps if I had a gun you might be able to read me better, but I haven't. You are quite right about one thing though; I suppose I am sending out signals even if I don't mean to.' She looked at him unblinkingly for a few moments before nodding and smiling. 'How would you like to earn a hundred dollars, Mr McNally?'

'Now what man in his right mind

wouldn't like to earn that much?' said Brogan. 'I have me this feelin' though that I ain't goin' to like what you want from me in return. You did say *earn* a hundred dollars.'

'Oh, it really is quite simple and well within your capabilities,' she said.

'Ma'am,' said Brogan with a deep sigh. 'Most folk go all their lives an' never shoot a man. In fact I've known many who hardly know how to use a gun. They just ain't never had cause to know how to. Me, I've been wanderin' since I was fourteen years old an' I reckon I'm well over fifty now, that's one hell of a long time an' I've had to learn a hell of a lot. I killed my first outlaw when I was fifteen an' I've killed more men than I care to count since that time. I don't kill for the sake of it, only if I have to. Neither do I steal anythin' from anyone. If I want money I have to work for it just like anyone else. Durin' that time I've learned that nothin' is just plain simple, nothin' at all. There's always a catch or a price to pay for even the simplest of things. Who do I have to kill to earn the money?'

'My brothers,' she replied simply, suddenly and almost disarmingly, giving him a big smile. It was almost as though she were asking him to rid her of vermin of some kind. It seemed that she thought of her brothers as vermin. 'In return for ridding me of them, I pay you one hundred dollars and I'll even let you hump me and not insist on you having a bath first. What more could a man want? A hundred dollars and my body. I don't give myself to just any man, you know.'

Brogan laughed loudly. 'Why is it that I'm not really surprised,' he said. 'I just ain't, that's all. The way you say it makes it sound almost reasonable, more like a business deal, which I suppose it is. Don't tell me the reason, I'll tell you. It's 'cos they stand to inherit your father's business before you do. The normal line of inheritance is through the male line. That's why most men want to sire sons, so's they can live on through them. In your case there's

47

three of them so the chances of all three of them dying of natural causes are well nigh impossible and if they marry and have children of their own that leaves you well down the list. So, if you want to take on the business, you have to eliminate them some other way and do it before they marry.'

'I couldn't have put it better myself,' she said.

'So, when I suddenly appear on the scene and seem able to outgun them, it's almost an answer to a prayer,' he said. 'Ma'am, you said earlier that you were not that desperate for a man to even think of me in that way — '

'I still am not,' she said. 'Let's just call it payment for services rendered, after you've killed them of course. Luke and Jed must have told you that I always honour my debts.'

'Sure, they told me,' agreed Brogan. 'Only thing is, I've got news for you too, Miss Betty. I'm not that desperate for a woman either, even one as pretty as you. As for your hundred dollars, if I was willin' to hire my gun, it would be at least one hundred dollars for each brother.'

'In Sulphur Springs I believe the going rate is fifty dollars a killing,' she said. 'Very well then, I'll match that. I'll make it one hundred and fifty dollars.'

'Ma'am,' said Brogan with a broad grin. 'If they charge fifty dollars in Sulphur Springs, then I suggest you get somebody from there to do it. My gun ain't for hire. Never has been, never will be.'

'You can have me right here and now,' she said, pushing her body close to him. 'I can assure you I know how to satisfy a man.'

'Sorry, Miss Betty,' he said. 'I reckon you sure do know how to pleasure a man, but this particular man's been around too long to expect any surprises. No deal, Miss Betty.'

She suddenly pouted. 'OK, OK, you win,' she hissed. 'Three hundred dollars, a hundred dollars each. I don't know where I am going to get it all but

I will, I can assure you of that.'

'No, ma'am,' Brogan replied firmly. 'OK, so I accept, then what happens? I'll tell you exactly what happens. Somehow your pa finds out I killed 'em an' he kills me or you even kill me yourself, the perfect solution. No jury would ever convict you of murder, it would be seen as justified. Either that or the law comes after me but that could raise a few questions you'd rather not have asked. Anyhow, I ain't never had the law after me in my life. I don't intend to start now.'

She suddenly relaxed and laughed.

'Very well, Mr McNally,' she said. 'It was worth a try. Many other men might have jumped at the chance to earn a hundred dollars or more. I obviously misjudged you.'

'I could tell your pa what you just said,' said Brogan.

'Go ahead,' she invited. 'It would be your word against mine and I do believe that mine would count for far more than that of a filthy old saddle bum.

Besides, I can twist my father round my little finger if I have to. Even if he does believe you, what is he going to do about it? I'll tell you, absolutely nothing. The same goes for my brothers. I've told them I'd like to see them all dead.'

'Ain't none of my business,' said Brogan. 'You can all shoot each other as far as I'm concerned. Just don't ask me to be part of it. Good day to you, Miss Betty. Don't worry, this conversation never took place.'

'I wasn't worrying, Mr McNally,' she said with a broad smile. 'I never worry about anything. There will be other times, possibly other saddle bums and other methods.'

3

Brogan wondered whether he should mention the incident with Betty Crossland to anyone else. He was uncertain whether anyone would believe him, particularly in view of the seemingly fairly high regard in which she was held. Even if they did, would they bother to do anything about it? There was, of course, the question as to exactly what they could do in any event. Thus far she had not actually done anything and, as far as he was aware, there were no laws being broken by her suggestion, even if he could prove she had made it.

Then again, there was absolutely no doubt that she would deny it and would probably claim it to be a vindictive reaction on his part. He was sufficiently experienced in the ways of women to realize that a well educated and intelligent woman, which Betty Crossland clearly was, would be able to twist things to make it appear that it was he who was at fault.

More than likely she would claim that he, Brogan McNally, had asked for, demanded or even tried to force a sexual relationship. It had happened to him before and he knew that a claim of rape or attempted rape was a very easy thing for a woman to make but a very difficult accusation for a man to disprove. For reasons he had never quite understood, it always appeared to be the woman who was believed and never the man. It was almost as if a woman would never lie about such things. However, he knew from experience that this was just not so.

There was also no doubt that she was quite highly thought of, particularly and understandably amongst the male population of Driftwood. As for the female population, he had had absolutely nothing to do with any of them so he simply did not know. In fact he had not seen more than three women during the short time he had been in the town and then only fleetingly.

He gave the matter some thought for a time but eventually decided that it was just not worth the bother and would achieve absolutely nothing as far as he was concerned. If a family wanted to wipe each other out, that was their affair, not his — just so long as it did not directly involve him. At that moment all he wanted was to get well away from Driftwood as soon as possible.

The condition of his horse was much improved and normally he would have risked riding her there and then. However, Luke Briscoe insisted that she was not quite right so he agreed to remain until the following day at least.

The remainder of that day passed without incident or visit from any of the Crosslands. In some strange way he had expected trouble in one form or another and from the three sons in particular, but was quite relieved when neither they, their father nor their sister put in an appearance.

The following morning the farrier, Luke Briscoe, was still not too happy about the condition of Brogan's horse but, when pressed, he was forced to concede that she could be ridden, providing she was not pushed too hard, given regular rests and that Brogan take some of the tincture to use on her. Brogan readily agreed, only too pleased at the prospect of at last being able to leave Driftwood.

★ ★ ★

Brogan had ridden into Driftwood from the south so, apart from returning that way, he had three main choices, east towards Fort Leveson, west towards Fort Kenyon or north. Since he had no particular desire to have any contact with the army, he decided that north and possibly Sulphur Springs was his only real option.

Sulphur Springs was apparently at

least five days' riding for most riders but the speed at which he and his horse usually travelled meant it would probably be closer to seven days or even longer. In any event, even five days was a long way and he could always take off in another direction whenever he chose and would probably do so at the first real opportunity. In his opinion, Sulphur Springs did not sound a good place to be — too much hot water. Brogan McNally and hot water did not agree.

About three hours after leaving Driftwood, Brogan suddenly had the sensation that he was being watched. At first it was little more than a feeling, but his feelings were rarely wrong and he *never* ignored them. He might well choose to do nothing but he never ignored his feelings and was always ready for action. He continued to ride slowly, keeping a constant look-out but without making it obvious.

After a fairly short time he could make out a lone figure astride a horse looking down on him from a ridge. Whoever it was blended in well with the brown, rocky background and even Brogan might not have noticed had it not been for the sudden movement of the horse and the flash of bright metal on the harness in the sunlight. There was no doubt in his mind that it was Betty Crossland. She made no attempt to hail or otherwise acknowledge him so he rode on, pretending that he had not seen her. An hour later he rested his horse alongside a small stream where he examined the hoof and applied some of the tincture.

Instinct and extra keen senses had kept Brogan alive on many occasions and in fact probably contributed more to his survival than his undoubted ability and speed with a gun. At that moment both senses and instinct were screaming at him.

There was no doubt about it, somebody was watching him. However, his senses also told him that it was Betty Crossland and that he was in no immediate danger. He remained seated on the ground but had his Colt resting between his legs just in case. There was the barely audible sound of a dry twig snapping underfoot but it was sufficient for Brogan's keen hearing.

'Afternoon, Miss Betty,' he called without turning.

'Good afternoon, Mr McNally,' came the immediate and plainly surprised response. 'I must say I'm impressed. How did you know I was here? I hardly made a sound.'

'You made enough noise to wake the dead,' said Brogan, grandly. 'I also seen you about an hour ago up on that ridge. It couldn't've been nobody else. What can I do for you? Don't bother to offer me more money to kill them brothers of yours either. You'd be wastin' your breath.'

'You saw me on the ridge?' she said. 'You must have sharp eyes. I deliberately kept in the cover of the rocks. At first I couldn't make out for certain if it was you or not. Anyway you never gave any indication that you had seen me.'

'Nope,' agreed Brogan. 'That way I get the edge. Now what can I do for you, Miss Betty? You sure ain't followed me all the way out here just to pass the time of day an' I don't suppose you've come all this way just for the ride. Does your pa own this land as well?'

'No, he does not,' she said. 'As a matter of fact I did follow you thinking I might be able to persuade you to change your mind. I was going to offer you two hundred dollars for each of my brothers.'

'Well you can't change my mind,' said Brogan. 'I already told you I ain't no hired killer. Saddle bum an' proud of it I might be, but I ain't never hired myself out as a killer an' never will. Oh, sure, I've helped out plenty of folk what really need some help an' I've often done it for free, but I ain't never hired myself out just to murder somebody. Looks like you've just wasted your time, Miss Betty. Seems to me you is gettin' pretty desperate.'

She sighed deeply and laughed drily.

'I am, Mr McNally,' she said. 'You see, the word is that my brother Jamie has put a girl from the town in the family way and that he's seriously considering doing the right thing by her and marrying her. I only know this because she told me so herself. She hasn't even told her mother or her father yet and Jamie doesn't know that I know.'

'Then it looks like you got yourself a problem if you want to take on the business,' said Brogan. 'Maybe you should talk to your pa about changin' his will. Ain't no concern of mine though.'

She smiled, dismounted and led her horse to the water alongside his horse, which placed her between the two horses. She picked up the hoof of Brogan's horse and looked briefly at it. She made some comment about it looking a lot better before resting her arm and chin on Brogan's saddle. She smiled invitingly at him for a while before suddenly shaking her head and laughing.

'I have talked to my father,' she said. 'He still insists that the boys have first chance. As far as he's concerned a woman's job is to have babies, cook and keep house and do whatever her husband tells her to do. OK, Mr McNally,' she said. 'I know when I'm beat. It was worth a try if nothing else.'

'If you think so, Miss Betty,' he said. 'Now, if you don't mind we'll be on our way, we got a long way to go.'

'We, Mr McNally?'

'Me an' her,' said Brogan, indicating his horse. 'Only female I ever been able to trust an' there've been plenty of times I didn't trust her either. Like all females, she's got a mind of her own.'

'You are very wise not to trust a woman.' She laughed. 'All females are devious and manipulative, it's in their nature. Not having the physical strength to get their own way, they learn it from the day they are born when the first thing they learn is that a sweet smile can twist their father round their fingers. Goodbye, Mr McNally, I don't suppose we shall ever meet again.'

Brogan did not reply as she mounted her horse and rode off. He watched as she slowly disappeared from view, the comment about all women being devious and manipulative ringing in his head. He was unable to put a finger on it, but he had the uneasy feeling that Betty Crossland had just been very devious and manipulative with him. He knew that the meeting had not been to persuade him to change his mind, there was much more to it. The only problem was that, although he knew that there must be one, he just could not come up with any logical explanation.

He made camp shortly before sunset, deliberately choosing a spot which gave him a commanding view of the surrounding country. For some reason he was very wary, more so than usual, but his concern apparently proved to be without reason. The night passed without incident.

The night might have passed without incident, but almost as soon as the first rays of light spread across the surrounding terrain, his ears picked up the sound of a horse being ridden very hard. His ears might have located the general direction of the sound but it was a few minutes before his eyes picked up the occasional tell-tale signs of dust.

A lone horseman — or possibly horsewoman, he could not tell which — was about a mile away and plainly intent on covering as much ground as possible. The way in which the horse was being ridden indicated to Brogan that whoever it was, was running away from something. He strained his eyes to look beyond the figure but was unable to see anyone in pursuit.

He shrugged, decided that whoever it was and for whatever reason they were fleeing, was no concern of his. He watched as horse and rider disappeared in the same direction as he was heading before he gathered his belongings and followed on.

After about another two hours he suddenly heard the sound of horses behind him. On this occasion it was obvious to him that there were several of them and it also seemed obvious that they were in pursuit of the rider he had seen earlier. However, anxious not to become involved, he decided to hide up behind a large group of rocks until they had ridden by. A few minutes later six horses and riders thundered past him.

He had the impression that the man leading the bunch was either an Indian or at least of Indian blood. He also had the impression that one of the riders was a woman. At first he thought of Betty Crossland but the horse she had been riding the previous day was most certainly not the same horse as the woman was riding. He was curious — very curious — but not sufficiently so to want to follow them and find out exactly what was happening. He waited for another half-hour before continuing his journey.

However, because there was so much

activity and because he was always cautious, Brogan chose not to follow the well-marked trail. Instead he followed along the slightly higher, wooded ground but parallel to the trail.

Shortly before midday, after travelling through fairly thick woodland, in which he felt quite safe, Brogan found himself looking down upon a wide river. There was an obvious ford where the trail crossed the river and it was also very plain that this ford was the only crossing point. Either side of it the river appeared to be very deep and was considerably wider. Upstream in particular seemed to be more like a small lake than a river.

Under normal circumstances Brogan would have simply ridden through but on this occasion, his senses were screaming at him that all was not as it appeared. For some time he remained where he was, atop a small hillock on the edge of the woods and overlooking the ford.

His instinct and senses had warned

him that something was not quite right and he very rarely dismissed such things. He studied both the approach to the ford and the far bank for some considerable length of time.

The approach to the ford presented no obvious problems. The ground was flat, treeless and virtually without cover of any kind. It would be almost impossible for anyone to ambush him on this side of the river. The opposite bank on the other hand was liberally covered with both large boulders and trees, ideal ambush country. Quite why he should believe that anyone would want to ambush him he did not really know. There was no logical reason for his feelings that he could think of but the feeling persisted and on this occasion, since he had time on his hands, he chose not to continue, which is what he often did despite the feelings. After about ten or fifteen minutes during which time he saw absolutely nothing which might have alerted him, Brogan still decided that his instincts could not be wrong.

For a few more minutes he discussed the situation with his horse. It was a typically one-sided conversation during which his horse either shook or nodded her head or gave the occasional snort. At the end of it all he apparently came to the conclusion that his horse agreed with him. However, his patience and caution appeared to be justified when for a brief moment, a man appeared at the edge of the woods and looked over the ford. He disappeared as quickly as he had arrived, but it was enough for Brogan.

'Only one thing for it, old girl,' he said to her. 'We go up river till we can find somewheres else to get across. It just ain't worth the risk. Whoever it is might be waitin' for that other rider, but they might just be waitin' for me. Anyhow, I reckon that other feller must be well past here by now. I sure ain't seen no sign of him hidin' anywheres.'

Keeping well in the cover of the forest, Brogan followed the river upstream for about another two hours. During that time he thought he saw various places where he might have crossed but he decided to continue upstream. Eventually he came to what was apparently an easy crossing point.

There was a series of large, flat rocks, most about thirty or forty feet wide, across the river, which at that point was almost twice as wide as it had been. Because the water-level was seemingly very low at that moment, it appeared to be an ideal crossing place. Had the water-level been even a little higher it would probably have been more difficult, which explained why it was not a regular ford. Once again, Brogan waited and studied. This time, however, he did not have the feeling of danger and after a short time decided it was safe to cross.

The actual crossing proved a little more difficult than he had anticipated. The channels between the large, flat rocks were all quite shallow and easy for his horse to negotiate — all except one. This one channel was the last and proved to be about twenty feet wide, apparently about six feet deep and very fast-flowing. He had been unable to see it from the bank; had he been able to do so he might have continued upstream. However, having made it this far, he was determined not to be beaten despite the prospect of a good soaking.

He moved upstream about twenty yards or so where he found a large, apparently deep pool. Here the water was much calmer and there were gentle slopes both into and out of the pool.

'OK, old girl,' he said to his horse. 'I guess some would say we both need a bath so we might as well count this as one. Don't know how deep the water is so I'll just have to hang on to you. I can't swim but I knows you can so I'm countin' on you. You ready?' The horse snorted and tossed her head. Brogan dismounted and led her forward. 'OK, let's go,' he said, pushing her forwards into the water.

Brogan had expected the water to be

cold, but it was a lot colder than anticipated. However, once in, his horse paddled forward whilst he clung to the saddle. After what was only in reality a very short time but which seemed a very long time to Brogan, both were clambering up and out of the river, Brogan gasping for breath even if his horse was not.

'Made it!' he gasped. 'Man, was that cold. First thing we do is light a fire an' dry out. Only hope I don't catch my death of cold.'

He soon had a large fire going, had stripped the saddle off his horse to allow her to dry out but had not taken any of his clothes off. He always preferred to let them dry on his body. It was only mid-afternoon but he decided that here was as good a place as any to stay for the night.

During the enforced swim his guns and some of his supplies had taken a thorough soaking. He spread the flour, sugar and salt on a large rock close to the fire to dry out in the hope that he might be able to save some of it. Then he set about oiling and cleaning his guns.

He always kept his guns in good condition, these and his wits were all he had and his life often depended on one or the other and often both. It was as he looked for the small bottle of oil he always carried for just such occasions that he made a strange discovery. In the bottom of one of his two saddlebags, he found what was plainly a gold brooch. The brooch itself was fairly large and thick and was obviously made of solid gold. He had seen enough gold in his time to realize that much. However, in the centre of it was a small cross made of brilliant, glasslike stones. He could only assume that the stones were diamonds.

'Now where in the hell did this come from?' he muttered to himself. 'I ain't never seen this before in my life.' He turned the brooch over and over, closely examining it for any clues. 'Nope, ain't never seen this thing before. Sure looks like pure gold though, must be worth a whole heap of money.' He tested it between his teeth although he really did not know why. He suddenly paused, raised his eyes thoughtfully to the skies and smiled slightly. 'I wonder?' he muttered again. 'I just wonder. Yeah, that must be it. But why?'

His thoughts had drifted back to the day before when Betty Crossland had laid her arms and chin on his saddle as she stared at him. He knew for certain that she had managed to put the brooch into his saddlebag. What he did not know was why. As far as he was concerned it simply did not make sense.

Then again there were other things which simply did not make sense as well, but he had chosen to ignore them. The first lone rider did not make any sense and the later riders also did not make any sense. At least they had not made sense up until that point. The group of riders, he now decided, were a posse and were apparently in pursuit of the lone rider. Who the lone rider was and why the posse should be in pursuit he had no idea. However, the more he thought about it, the more convinced he was that the two were not connected. The posse was in search of him, not the lone rider.

That might well have explained those particular incidents but it most certainly did not explain why Betty Crossland had placed the brooch in his saddlebag. Neither did it explain the very strong feelings he had had about crossing the ford but then he could never explain his instincts.

He was still quite convinced that he had been right about not crossing the ford but it did not explain a thing. He now definitely did not believe that the posse was waiting for the strange, lone rider. He believed they were waiting for him — but why?

He set about cleaning and oiling his guns and tried to make sense of the situation. He failed miserably.

However, it appeared that his detour had thrown them off. He climbed a small hill which gave him a good view downstream. There was no sign of anyone and a close study of the trees did not indicate any strange or unusual presence. Had there been anyone there, the birds would have taken flight as they approached.

The flight of birds was always a good indicator of progress of men and horses. Birds did not take flight at the sight of normal happenings such as deer, bears or wolves but, for some strange reason, they almost always took flight at the sight of man and groups of men in particular. Even so he listened.

Eventually he was satisfied and returned to his camp. He managed to salvage most of the salt, which somehow had escaped the worst of the soaking. The flour was beyond saving, having been transformed into lumps of dough. The sugar had congealed into crystaline lumps but was still usable.

His other supplies being more solid, had escaped with nothing more than getting wet.

That night passed without incident.

4

Although the night had passed without incident, Brogan was still very wary. It was not that his senses and instincts were telling him anything, they were not, it was more that he was being ultra cautious. Before leaving he once again climbed the small hill and looked down river. There was no sign of anything or anyone and eventually he was satisfied that it was nothing more than his imagination working overtime. There was nothing unusual in that, it often did, but it got in the way of his natural feelings and senses on occasion.

After a fairly short time travelling, he cleared the forested area along the river and found himself looking across a rolling plain liberally covered in vegetation and rocky outcrops. The rolling nature of the land and the many columns of rock made it impossible to see any great detail close to for the most part. However, there were one or two more elevated places where he did have a good view for miles around. Even then, had anyone or anything been in one of the many hollows or amongst the rocks he would never have seen them.

Further to the west, he guessed about ten miles away, there was what seemed to be almost sheer-sided mountains rising many hundreds of feet. To the east, in the far distance, he could just make out snow-covered peaks of other mountains. The fact that they were covered in snow told him that they were even higher than those to the west. He appeared to have little choice but to keep heading north.

At about midday he came across a large pool of good, clear water set amongst a circle of rocks. Up to that point what few water holes he had seen had been quite small and rather unappetizing looking in that they were covered in green slime. Since neither time nor distance meant a great deal to

Brogan, he decided to rest himself and his horse for a while in the shade of a large tree.

Unusually for Brogan, he seemed to have fallen asleep. Suddenly he was wide awake and grabbing at his gun but he was too late. It appeared that this was one of those few occasions when his senses and instincts had failed him. Even when asleep he usually sensed when things were not right. On this occasion he found himself looking into the barrel of a rifle held by an Indian.

'Afternoon,' he said, rather weakly and feeling very foolish at his lapse of concentration. 'Want somethin'?'

'I think I have found what I was looking for,' replied the Indian in perfect English. 'Mr Brogan McNally I believe.'

'The very same,' replied Brogan. 'What can I do for you?'

'You can come back with us to Driftwood,' said the Indian.

'What the hell for?' asked Brogan. 'An' just who the hell is *us*?'

'*Us* is a posse formed to track you down,' replied another voice. The figure of Luke Briscoe stepped from behind a big rock. He aimed a large, powerful buffalo rifle at Brogan. 'Don't even think about using that gun, Mr McNally,' he continued, raising the gun slightly to reinforce his point. 'I might not be a gunfighter but even I can't miss from here with this thing.'

'A gun like that would probably blow my head clean off from that distance,' agreed Brogan. 'Ah yes, I saw you ride by. I saw you waitin' down by that ford across the river as well. Somethin' told me you was lookin' for me but for the life of me I couldn't work out why an' I still can't. I thought I saw a woman with you. I take it that was Betty Crossland.'

'Very observant, Mr McNally,' said Betty Crossland following Luke Briscoe from behind the rock. Three other men also appeared from close by. 'I'm surprised we were able to get to you so easily. I had expected you to put up a 'fight and for you to be killed.'

'What you really mean is you'd hoped I'd be killed, Miss Betty,' muttered Brogan. 'I'm surprised too, about you gettin' to me so easy, that is. I must be gettin' old, I don't usually fall asleep in the middle of the day.' He looked at the Indian and smiled. 'Now I see why you're with 'em,' he said to him. 'You probably know all about trackin' folk. If it had just been this lot they'd never've got within a mile of me, even when I was asleep. Now would somebody mind tellin' me just what this is all about?'

'You know darned well what this is all about,' snarled Luke Briscoe. 'You murdered Sam Crossland an' two of his boys, Jamie and Nathan. The youngest, Jonathan, is missin' too. What you done with him?'

Brogan could not help but laugh.

'I am *definitely* gettin' old,' he said. 'I should have figured you'd do somethin' like this, Miss Betty.' He laughed again. 'It ain't me you want for them murders,

Mr Briscoe, if you want anybody it's Miss Betty here more'n like.'

'Are you sayin' Miss Betty murdered her own pa an' brothers?' sneered Luke Briscoe. 'I don't think so, McNally. What the hell would she want to do a thing like that for?'

'To get her hands on the ranch,' said Brogan. 'It must have been very convenient havin' somebody like me ride through Driftwood, the answer to a prayer, you might say. I don't suppose she told you she offered me money to kill her brothers did she? Naw, she would never admit somethin' like that but take it from me, that's just what she did. I guess she just took it a step further. Didn't say nothin' about killin' her pa though, I gotta admit that.'

They all looked sharply at Betty Crossland, at each other and Luke Briscoe nervously licked his lips.

'I knew he'd try to shift the blame,' said Betty Crossland with a nervous laugh. 'What else would you expect him to say? He has to cover himself, doesn't he, so he tries to put the blame on me. Do you really think I would ask a complete stranger to commit murder for me? I can assure you I could hire more reliable men in Sulphur Springs. You all must know that. Anyway I think I can prove it was him. I told you he stole a valuable, solid-gold and diamond brooch. It was on a dresser near where he killed my father. You know what it looks like, Luke. Search him and his things, I'll guarantee it's there somewhere. Let's see if he can explain that away.'

'Now it all begins to make sense,' said Brogan. 'I gotta hand it to you, Miss Betty, you seem to have it all figured out. Go ahead, look where you've a mind to look. You won't find nothin'.'

Luke Briscoe nodded to one of the other men who searched through Brogan's saddlebags and bedroll. There was no sign of the brooch. Brogan smiled as he noted the alarmed look on Betty Crossland's face. The man also searched Brogan but once again there was no sign of the brooch.

'What have you done with it?' she demanded. 'I know you took it.'

'Then you know a darned sight more'n I do,' said Brogan. 'If I had stolen it I sure ain't had time to sell it nowheres have I? Speakin' of time, take a look at my old horse. You know her pretty well, Mr Briscoe. Do you reckon I've had time to kill Miss Betty's pa an' brothers an' get this far on that old horse? She's got a lame foot, you know that, an' can't be driven hard. If I had ridden her hard, and I would have to have done just that to get this far in the time, I'd say her foot would've been real bad by now, wouldn't you? Even if she hadn't been lame she sure ain't the fastest horse there is. She's almost as old as I am. Takes her all her time to put one leg in front of the other most of the time. I must've left Driftwood a good day or more before they was murdered from what I can make out. You all know how fast you had to ride to get this far an' you probably started out soon after the killin's was discovered. That would mean I must've left not that long before you did. Can you really see my old horse bein' able to do that?'

Luke Briscoe looked hard at Brogan for a few moments and then at Betty Crossland. He picked up the hoof of Brogan's horse and examined it closely. He shook his head as he spoke to Betty Crossland.

'What he says makes sense,' he said to her. 'This horse sure hasn't been ridden hard, I'll guarantee that. Thing is as well, nobody actually saw him at your place, not even you. All we have to go on is your word. It could've been anyone, includin' me, I reckon. Most folk would be unable to account for where they were at the time. We all just assumed it must've been him. We haven't found the brooch either. Sure, that would've clinched it but he hasn't got it. Are you sure it was stolen? Maybe it was knocked off the dresser or somethin', or your ma moved it.'

'He must have stolen it,' she insisted. 'It was definitely on the dresser, my mother will confirm that. That was where it was always kept and she is not in the habit of moving things and then forgetting.'

'Well he hasn't got it,' said the man who had searched both saddlebags and Brogan. He looked in the saddlebags once again and even poked a knife among the coffee beans and salt and emptied the sugar — now in lumps — on to the ground despite Brogan's protests but he eventually shook his head. 'Nope, definitely not here, Miss Betty.'

'It has to be there somewhere,' she almost screamed as she leapt forward and searched the saddlebags herself. The other man also searched Brogan again. 'What have you done with it?' she shouted when she found nothing more than his supplies, two boxes of bullets, a spyglass and a few bits and pieces Brogan had collected over the years.

'Why did you deliberately avoid us?' she demanded. 'If you are innocent, as you claim to be, why try to avoid us?'

'Because I don't like people very much,' said Brogan. 'I prefer my own company, at least I can trust myself. People are always tryin' to make trouble for me for some strange reason, just like you are doin' now. OK, Mr Briscoe, you seem to be in charge, you ain't found nothin' an' you agree I could never've made it this far if I had killed her pa an' brothers, what you goin' to do now?'

'We take him back and let the judge decide,' shouted Betty Crossland.

'Only trouble is we ain't got one bit of proof,' said Luke Briscoe. He turned to the others. 'What do you think?'

'You're right,' said one, 'I ain't doubtin' Miss Betty for one moment an' she probably really believes he did kill them, but when it comes down to it it's just her word — '

'And whose word would you rather believe, Jim Mossman,' shouted Betty Crossland. 'Mine or the word of a filthy old saddle tramp?'

'It ain't a matter of believin' one or the other,' replied the man. 'I worked for a lawyer for many years so I know a few things about the law. We just ain't got no cause to hold him. I say we ain't got no choice but to let him go.'

'Then shoot him right here,' hissed Betty Crossland. 'Nobody will ever ask any questions, he's nothing but a stinking saddle tramp and nobody gives a damn what happens to saddle tramps.'

'But we'd all know, Miss Betty,' said Luke. 'We're not killers or gunmen, we're farmers, storekeepers and suchlike. I know if we killed him I'd never be able to live with it on my conscience.'

'A pox on you and your conscience,' she snarled. 'You haven't got a backbone between the lot of you.'

'If you say so, Miss Betty,' sighed Luke Briscoe. 'OK, you can go, McNally. Just do yourself a favour an' never come back this way again. Folk hereabouts have mighty long memories and others might not be as reasonable as we are.'

'I reckon if you find her other brother, Jonathan I think he's called, you'll soon discover the truth of it,' said Brogan. 'What say you, Miss Betty?'

'I think that he somehow escaped from you but followed you,' she said. 'He was only a boy and no match for you. You probably dumped his body somewhere. There's thousands of places he could be.'

'Can't be sure of that though, can you?' said Brogan with a broad grin. 'I reckon you need Jonathan to be dead. He's probably the only other person who knows the truth of what happened. I *can* tell you that somebody who looked a lot like your brother was ridin' like the devil himself was after him not that long before I first saw you. I made the mistake of thinking you were chasing him.'

'There were signs of a pony at the river crossing,' said the Indian. 'I told you about it at the time. You said not to bother since it was a pony and McNally's horse sure don't fall into that category. It could've been Jonathan. I know he always preferred ridin' that pony of his to a horse.'

Brogan grinned. 'Find the brother, you find the killer.'

'Are you sayin' he killed 'em?' asked Briscoe.

'No, all I'm sayin' is find him an' you'll find your murderer,' said Brogan. 'I'm just a bit curious as to why or how you managed to find me up here?'

'I found your tracks on the edge of the forest,' said the Indian. 'I know this land, I was born and raised here. There were only a few places for you to cross the river without having to swim and I do not think you are a man who likes water too much. It was easy to find out just where you crossed. All I had to do was follow the river upstream until I found the signs. When I did there were so many of them even a blind man could have seen them.'

'I guess so,' agreed Brogan. 'You're right about me not likin' water but I had to swim an' took one hell of a soakin'. I didn't even think about leavin' signs. It didn't seem important at the time. OK, I'll be on my way. I sure hope you find who murdered 'em pretty soon but you ain't got far to look if I'm any judge. I think I've already told you, I ain't never murdered nobody in my life. I've killed a few, that's for sure, but they always asked for it. Maybe the law wouldn't always see it that way but at least my conscience is clear.'

Brogan mounted his horse and urged it into a trot. He was about twenty yards from them when Betty Crossland suddenly screamed out.

'You can't let him go! He murdered my father and my brothers. He has to die for it.'

'Sorry, Miss Betty,' said Luke Briscoe. 'We don't believe he did it.'

'Bastard!' she yelled at Brogan. 'Don't think you've got away with this.

I intend to see that you pay for it if it's the last thing I do. I sent a wire to the marshal, I've arranged to meet him. These fools didn't know I'd sent for him but when I see him I know he won't just stand by like this lily-livered lot. They're all too scared of their own shadows to do anything when it comes down to it.' She turned on Luke Briscoe. 'As for you, I'll make sure you never work for me again'. She called out to Brogan again. 'There's nowhere you can ride now, McNally.'

Brogan did not even look back as he rode away but he had certainly heard every word she had said and he was not very happy. One of the things he prided himself on was that he had never been a wanted man — in effect an outlaw — and he did not relish the idea of becoming one now. He was quite certain that Betty Crossland would be able to persuade any lawman that he, Brogan McNally, had committed almost any crime. He rode on, pondering his position and turning over various alternative plans of action in his mind.

He was very thankful that he had not kept the brooch. It might well have been very valuable but it was far too distinctive for him to attempt to sell it. Descriptions and pictures of stolen jewellery were constantly circulated and most dealers had one. At the time he had not known why Betty Crossland should put it into his saddlebag and he *had* been tempted to keep it. Now he knew the answer.

At least by throwing it into the river he had saved himself having to face a trial, an almost certain hanging and quite possibly a lynching instead of a trial. Betty Crossland would somehow have seen to that, she definitely could not afford for him to tell what he knew in open court even if he was not believed. He was also quite certain that he had not seen or heard the last of Betty Crossland, either directly, or indirectly in the form of a US marshal.

He rode until shortly before sunset,

all the time listening and watching for signs of being followed. However, there was none, he was quite certain of that. The only member of the posse who might have been able to follow without being detected was the Indian and he did not think that he was following. Knowing that the Indian just might get close to him again, he had taken extra care.

He eventually made camp alongside a small, clear stream situated on high ground overlooking the narrow valley along which he had been travelling. He had a clear view in all directions but, after spending a long time looking and even listening, he was satisfied that he had not been followed.

There were few happenings or situations which really bothered Brogan, he was able to shrug off most things but the thought of being pursued by a US marshal had him really worried. His experience of men like that was not very good. Most, he had discovered, were so single minded that it was impossible to talk to them. The very fact that they were in pursuit of a man was enough to mean that he was guilty in their eyes. Nor was it at all unusual for a marshal to kill his quarry even when there was no need. Doing so usually made for an easier life and questions were very rarely asked of the marshal.

The more he thought about it, the more concerned he became and eventually decided that the only way he would ever be able to clear his name would be to locate the missing Crossland brother, Jonathan, before anyone else could do so, particularly the boy's sister, Betty. He was wise enough to know that Betty Crossland would not let matters rest solely with the marshal. She too, if not actually searching herself, would have people looking for her brother. She simply could not afford for him to remain at large and alive.

The night passed without incident and by the time the sun had risen Brogan had decided that the best chance he had of finding the boy was to head for Sulphur Springs. In his experience youths on the run tended to head for the nearest large town.

He headed across country to rejoin the main trail. Later that day he came across a trading post and took the opportunity to rest and replace his supply of flour and sugar. Whilst there he idly asked if anyone had passed that way in the past day or two.

He was told that a boy of about fifteen years had stopped briefly two or three days earlier — the owner could not be certain — and that a solitary woman had passed through the previous day. It seemed that she was also interested in the whereabouts of the boy, claiming that he was her brother. Brogan confirmed that that was indeed the case.

He was somehow not at all surprised to hear that Betty Crossland had passed that way, he was just surprised that it had happened so soon. Against that, he should have guessed that the only place a marshal might be found was at Sulphur Springs.

★ ★ ★

It took Brogan another four and a half days to reach the city of Sulphur Springs. He had not pushed his horse despite the urgency involved, that was not Brogan's way of working.

His first sighting of the city was from a high ridge. There appeared to be a haze covering most of the city which was especially dense towards the east and even Brogan knew this was due to the steady rise of steam from several pools of water. There were also at least two geysers — something which Brogan had seen once before, many years previously. There appeared to be a railroad crossing east to west. It was a large city with a great many streets and a large population, all of whom, from his vantage point, scuttled about like so many ants.

He was in no great hurry to enter the

city. Quite apart from the fact that he did not like too many people around him, he was trying to work out where things were.

The main centre of activity seemed centred on the railroad station which occupied a site slightly to the north. There he would no doubt find the better hotels, the civic offices and, more importantly as far as he was concerned, the marshal's office. A city of this size would probably have, in addition, a sheriff's or town constable's office and, if previous experience was anything to go by, each would jealously guard their own sphere of influence.

Also, somewhere amongst the warren of streets and teeming masses, was Betty Crossland. It was also possible that Jonathan Crossland was there somewhere but he would be more difficult to find. It was fairly easy for a boy to become lost in the crowd. Few people would notice a lone boy. Towns the size of Sulphur Springs attracted a large population of boys and young men who had left home for one reason or another. There was little reason for anyone to remember any one particular boy.

There was another reason why Brogan was interested in the layout of the city; he was looking for a likely spot to spend the night. He tried to avoid hotels and rooming-houses where possible, preferring to sleep out in the open. To the west of the city there was a wide river along which there appeared to be clumps of trees. He decided to investigate further.

He had been right about the clumps of trees, but he soon discovered that most of them had houses built amongst them. They were plainly the houses of the more affluent people of Sulphur Springs and none except one offered any shelter. The exception also had a building but it was obviously unused and in need of repair. Brogan decided that it was the perfect place. Judging by the state of the place it was apparent that he was not the first itinerant to use it.

By that time it was getting late and he decided to stay where he was for the night and start looking for Jonathan Crossland in the morning. He had just cooked himself a meal when he heard someone approaching. From the noise being made he thought it must be at least three men but in the event it turned out to be one lone drunk.

'Hi there!' slurred the drunk when he saw Brogan. He did not appear too surprised. 'This is my bunk but you're welcome to share.' He sniffed the air and licked his lips. 'I smell food,' he slurred again. 'I ain't eaten a decent meal in three days.'

'There's a bit left,' said Brogan, pushing his pot towards the man. 'You're welcome to it. Not much though, beans an' salt beef. I ain't much of a cook.'

'Beans an' salt beef sounds fine by me,' said the drunk. 'Thanks, neighbour.' He flopped down beside Brogan and grabbed at the pot, apparently oblivious as to how hot it was. 'What brings you to this hell-hole?' he asked through a mouthful of food. 'I see you got a horse.' He took another mouthful. 'I had me a horse once, 'bout a year ago. Lost her in a poker-game. Cheated out of it I was. There I was sittin' with a full house of three sevens an' two kings an' this feller produces four queens. Now I knows that was impossible since I'd just discarded one of them queens.' He took another mouthful. 'Didn't make no difference though, other three players were in it with him. The law don't recognize gamblin' debts round these parts an' said it was my own fault. Lost my gun the same way.' He looked blearily at Brogan's gun. 'You hang on to both your gun an' your horse, mister. Folk like you an' me allus need a horse an' a gun.'

'I never gamble', said Brogan. 'I never drink much either. I like to have my wits about me.'

'Then all I can say is your life must be bloody dull,' said the drunk with a broad grin. 'Me, I like gamblin', drinkin' an' women. Only trouble is it ain't often I gets the chance to do all three at once. Still, maybe that's all about to change. I reckon I found me a real gold mine an' right now she's sittin' up in the Hotel Metropole.'

'She likes a bit of rough does she?' asked Brogan, not really interested.

'Rough! Naw, it ain't nothin' like that,' slurred the drunk. 'A woman like that wouldn't look twice at me for somethin' like that. I know her from a few years ago out at a place called Driftwood. Yeah, Driftwood. Ain't that one hell of a name for a town?'

Suddenly Brogan was very interested in what the drunk had to say.

5

'So what does this woman want?'
Brogan asked as casually as possible,
not wanting to appear too interested. 'It
must be somethin' mighty important if
you think she's goin' to pay you well for
any information you come up with.'

'I didn't say nothin' about no information,' grunted the drunk. 'How'd you
know that? I never said nothin'.'

'It just seemed the logical thing,' said
Brogan, realizing that the drunk was
not quite as dense or possibly even as
drunk as he appeared. 'From experience I've learned that most women hire
men like you an' me either to kill
somebody or to find out where
somebody is. I don't think she would
have hired you to kill anybody for her
so that leaves findin' out where
somebody is.'

'You got a lot of experience then?'

grunted the drunk.

'Enough,' said Brogan. 'Let's just say I've had dealin's with women like that before. Anyhow, since you say you knew her in this Driftwood place, I'd say it's got somethin' to do with there. She probably thinks you know somebody from there who she wants to find. It also seems to me that because she's hirin' somebody like you an' not goin' to the sheriff to find out, she doesn't want the law involved. Don't it make you wonder why?'

The drunk looked at Brogan and sneered. 'Regular know-all ain't you?' he drawled. 'I don't know yet for sure who she wants or why she wants me to find him but if you is lookin' for a piece of action you can forget it. I ain't sharin' nothin' with nobody.'

'OK, it's your business,' said Brogan. 'Me, I got other things on my mind.'

The other things included finding somewhere else to stay for the night. He preferred to be on his own. Although he was quite certain that he could deal with anything the drunk might attempt, he did not particularly want to be bothered. That apart, he felt that the drunk might be more than useful in locating Jonathan Crossland for him as well as for Betty Crossland. The only thing of which he was reasonably certain was that the drunk might well attempt to rob him during the night and he might have to kill him. The drunk was far more use to him alive.

Much to the apparent amusement and many coarse comments of the drunk, Brogan collected his belongings and left to find somewhere else. He did find a tumbledown shack alongside the river about 200 yards away.

* * *

Brogan was awake and sitting outside his shack and keeping watch for the drunk as soon as the first rays of morning sun crept across the open ground between the river and the town. Brogan might have been wide awake but it appeared that the drunk was most definitely not an early riser. In fact it was almost midday before he put in an appearance.

He emerged from the building alternately yawning, coughing and spitting. He stretched his arms high and then proceeded to give himself a good scratch. Brogan knew full well the irresistible urge to scratch and de-bug himself. He had done so very frequently. Eventually the drunk went down to the river and immersed his head. Like Brogan, that appeared to be the full extent of his ablutions.

The drunk had claimed that he did not own a horse and Brogan had already decided that the only way to follow him was on foot. He had no worries about anyone stealing his horse, she was certainly not a prime animal and he knew that she would be most awkward with anyone who did try. Not wanting to carry his rifle, he found what he considered to be a safe hiding-place for it. He looked at the ancient saddle, cooking utensils and bedroll and decided that he had little choice but to hide them as best he could and chance their being discovered by someone desperate enough to want to steal them.

The drunk headed towards the railroad station and the Hotel Metropole. Brogan remained outside a saloon on the opposite side of the square and watched while the drunk removed his battered hat and went inside the hotel.

He was ushered out almost immediately and very unceremoniously by a very large and rather formidable-looking woman and apparently given strict instructions to remain on the boardwalk. The woman said something else to him and then disappeared. A few minutes later she reappeared with another younger woman. There was no mistaking Betty Crossland.

After a few minutes, Betty Crossland returned inside the hotel and the drunk crossed the square heading straight for Brogan. There seemed little point in hiding, or attempting to avoid him so

Brogan leant against a rail and waited. In the event, it seemed that the drunk had not recognized him as he simply ignored him, walked past and headed down a side street. Brogan followed at what he considered a safe distance behind.

As far as Brogan was concerned, the remainder of the day was for the most part a complete waste of time. He had assumed that the drunk had been given instructions to find Jonathan Crossland but he appeared to be going about it in a most peculiar way.

It appeared that the drunk's search was also a waste of time since he did not, apparently, find the boy. That, however, was hardly surprising since all he did was go from saloon to saloon and Brogan did not believe that a fifteen-year-old boy would frequent such places.

Brogan's enforced journey around the streets of Sulphur Springs did, however, serve one useful purpose. During the day he located the sheriff's office, the marshal's office, most of the saloons, whorehouses and gaming-houses. He learned that the sheriff was one Michael Seaton and, more importantly as far as he was concerned, that the marshal was named James Simpson. He wondered if Betty Crossland had yet spoken to the marshal. He also began to wonder if she ever would.

There was no doubt that the murders of her father and brothers would have to be reported and he had little doubt that she would attempt to blame him for those murders. He was, however, now more convinced than ever that finding the remaining brother was more important then sending the marshal in search of him. There was no doubt in his mind that eliminating Jonathan Crossland was her priority.

After a time it occurred to Brogan that the drunk was not actually looking for Jonathan Crossland but asking questions of likely people. He did not, apparently, find the answer to any of his questions. The drunk drifted from one saloon to another having one drink in each establishment but even with only one drink in each saloon, there were more than enough saloons for the effects of the beer to rapidly take its toll on the condition of the drunk.

It was not too long before even the shortest of walks between saloons took longer and longer and the drunk found it increasingly difficult to negotiate the steps of the boardwalks. Eventually, in the late afternoon, the alcohol took complete control and the drunk ended face down in a gutter with a deputy sheriff bearing down on him.

'I wouldn't waste your time with him,' said Brogan, reaching the body of the drunk just before the deputy. 'I knows where he's beddin' down. I'll take him off the streets for you.'

'Friend of yours?' grunted the deputy. 'Didn't think he had any friends.'

'No, not a friend,' said Brogan. 'I only met him last night. I guess you could say I just took pity on him.'

'Suits me,' said the deputy. 'I got

better things to do with my time than take trash like him into jail every day. He can never pay the fine anyhow. Just get him out of my sight and tell him to keep off the streets.'

'Sure thing,' agreed Brogan. 'He tells me he was lookin' for somebody, a boy aged fifteen, Jonathan Crossland I think he's called.'

'Well he sure won't find no fifteen-year-old in the bars or saloons,' said the sheriff. 'We got laws in this city against minors drinkin' alcohol in public.'

'An' a good thing too,' said Brogan. 'I don't suppose you've got any idea where I might find a lone fifteen-year-old boy?'

'Nope, don't take much notice of things like that,' said the deputy. 'There's sometimes a few lads hang about outside the lumber yard on the north side of town. I think some of them are on their own. They're lookin' for work an' the lumber yard has casual jobs from time to time.'

'Thanks, I'll try there,' said Brogan.

The deputy kicked the body of the drunk, laughed and went on his way. Brogan managed to get the drunk to his feet and, supporting him under one shoulder, eventually found his way back to the river. There seemed little point in attempting to talk to the drunk so Brogan laid him out on his makeshift bed and returned to his own shack. His horse and belongings had not been touched.

The following morning he checked on the drunk, found that he was still unconscious and decided to head for the lumber yard. He did not hold out much hope of finding Jonathan Crossland and did not think that he would be looking for work but it was as good a place as any to make a start. He would probably gravitate towards boys of his own age and it was always possible that one of them might know of him.

There were five youths outside the lumber gates and although Brogan had only seen Jonathan Crossland very briefly he was reasonably certain that he would recognize him again. He was not one of the five, of that he was quite certain. He decided to ask the youths if they knew of Jonathan.

Four of them shook their heads and Brogan believed them. The fifth smirked, looked Brogan straight in the face and then slowly turned his head slightly to spit on the ground.

'Information costs money,' he drawled, straightening himself up and puffing his chest out. 'What you want him for anyhow?'

'That's between him an' me,' said Brogan. 'Do you know him or not? He can't have been in town all that long.'

'Five dollars,' said the youth. 'I reckon that kind of information is worth five dollars of anybody's money.'

'It ain't worth a piece of dog-shit,' hissed Brogan, resisting the temptation to slam his fist into the boy's sneering face. 'Don't waste my time, boy,' he continued. 'You don't know nothin'.'

He turned and walked away from the youths but he did not walk very far. He found a narrow alley from where he could still see the youths. A short time later a man came out of the lumber yard, spoke to them and one of them ran inside. It seemed that he had struck lucky. The other four looked disheartened and ambled away, three of them together but the sneering youth left alone.

Brogan followed him along several streets until he disappeared inside what seemed to be a derelict building on the edge of town. He waited for a few minutes when suddenly Jonathan Crossland appeared. He looked wildly about and raced off before Brogan could attract his attention, although he doubted if it would have made any difference had he done so. It appeared that the sneering youth had told Jonathan that he was looking for him.

Although he had only seen him once and for a fairly short period, Brogan was quite certain that it had been Jonathan Crossland. There was little point in attempting to follow him, he had too much of a start and that particular part of town was a warren of narrow streets and alleyways among which anyone could easily become lost. However, at least he knew for certain that Jonathan Crossland was in town. All he had to do was get to the boy before his sister could.

As he was about to turn down another side street, the sneering youth emerged but apparently did not see Brogan. Out of nothing more than idle curiosity, Brogan decided to follow him again.

He did not have to follow the youth too far and he ended up outside one of the many saloons, although this particular one was more run-down than most. The youth briefly stepped inside and a short time later came out with two surly-looking men. The men appeared to listen to what the youth had to say but whatever he had to tell them did not seem to interest them all that much as one of them roughly pushed the youth off the boardwalk. Both men laughed coarsely and went back inside the saloon. The youth made an obscene gesture, unseen by either of them, picked himself up and slowly ambled down an alleyway.

Brogan was quite certain that the youth had told the two men what had happened and he was uncertain as to whether or not the information would be of interest. He decided to hang about.

Suddenly and rather unexpectedly, his wait was rewarded by the arrival of the drunk. Brogan was very surprised; it was not yet midday and appeared far too early for him to be about but there he was. He disappeared inside the saloon. A few minutes later he came out in the company of the two men Brogan had seen earlier. A few words were exchanged which became a little heated and the drunk stomped off along the boardwalk. The two men followed a few yards behind and Brogan shadowed them from the opposite side of the street.

As the trio passed a narrow alley, the

drunk was suddenly dragged along it and it was plain from the cries that he was being beaten. Brogan chose not to interfere for the moment. A few minutes later the two men appeared looking rather pleased with themselves and returned to the saloon. Brogan crossed the street and went down the alleyway.

There was no doubt about it, the drunk was dead. The fact that his head had been almost severed from his body by a large, very deep gash in his neck was enough to tell anyone what had happened. At that moment, the last thing Brogan needed was to be accused of murdering anyone else so he disappeared down the alley and along the backs of several properties. He was apparently unseen. He had the feeling that the drunk had been forced to tell all he knew before he had been killed.

The fate of the drunk was the last thing on Brogan's mind at that moment. He was very concerned that Jonathan Crossland might suffer a similar end and, far more importantly, concerned that *he* might well be accused of the boy's murder.

His presence in Sulphur Springs and Driftwood, the murders of the other Crosslands and the possible murder of Jonathan would be seen as too much of a coincidence by most lawmen. His concern was highlighted later that afternoon when he saw Betty Crossland crossing the street and entering the marshal's office. As far as he was concerned there was only one possible reason for her visit which meant that now more than ever, he had to find Jonathan Crossland.

When Betty Crossland left the marshal's office, Brogan followed her. Quite why he did so he was not certain but when she reached her hotel the two men who had murdered the drunk were waiting for her. They talked for a while outside the hotel until eventually, to the obvious disgust of the large woman, Betty Crossland invited them inside. After about half an hour they emerged looking quite pleased with themselves.

Once again, for reasons best known to himself at the time, Brogan followed them and was not at all surprised when they ended up at the tumbledown building where the sneering youth apparently lived. The youth was dragged out and slapped about the face a couple of times by one of the men. Brogan smiled, the men were obviously persuading the youth to find Jonathan Crossland for them. Eventually the men left in one direction and the youth in another. Brogan decided to follow the youth.

However, although the youth led Brogan all over town, there was no sign of Jonathan Crossland.

The deputy sheriff recognized Brogan as both men met. Mainly because he was not expecting trouble, Brogan was unable to react when the deputy suddenly produced his gun and aimed it at Brogan.

'I reckon you got a few questions to answer,' hissed the deputy, reaching forward and removing Brogan's gun.

'Turn round an' keep movin',' he ordered. 'Don't think I won't kill you if you try anythin' either, gun or no gun. We found the body of your friend.'

'I suppose it was only a matter of time,' said Brogan, doing as he was told. 'Only thing is he warn't no friend of mine an' it wasn't me what killed him. What the hell would I want to do somethin' like that for?'

'How the hell should I know? You can tell the sheriff all about it,' said the deputy. 'All I know is it was you who picked him up out of the gutter. You reckoned you knew him, now he's dead. I reckon you do have a few questions to answer. You can sort it out with the sheriff.'

The sheriff, Michael Seaton, looked up at Brogan and wrinkled his nose as he sniffed.

'You stink,' he muttered. 'Your type usually do.' He looked Brogan up and down and nodded. 'Saddle bum,' he declared. 'Got it written all over you. I've had me lots of dealin's with saddle bums an' I ain't met a decent one yet. Most would skin a turd if they thought there was any money in it. So why did you murder Lester Davidson?'

'I never knew his name,' said Brogan. 'I didn't murder him either.'

'You seem to know him well enough,' said the sheriff. 'My deputy tells me it was you who picked him out of the gutter. Why did you do that? An' what would you say if I told you I'd got me a witness who saw you goin' down the alley where the body was found?'

'I'd tell you your witness got it wrong,' said Brogan. 'Things ain't quite what they seem. Sure, I went down that alley an' I admit I found his body an' pretty messy it was too. Throat slit from ear to ear — '

'The jails are full of folk who claim a witness got it wrong,' said the sheriff. 'Only thing is I don't think every witness gets it wrong every time. I wish I had five dollars every time I heard somebody tell me things ain't quite what they seem, I'd be a rich man now.

Sure, I'll admit there's folk been sent to prison an' even hanged 'cos a witness got it wrong, but it don't happen that often. The thing is if you *are* innocent and you found his body why didn't you report it?'

Brogan had to admit to himself that his predicament looked very black. He appeared to have two choices, either tell the sheriff the truth or try to lie his way out of it.

The truth would obviously have been the better option had the truth been different. As it was, he believed that telling the truth would achieve nothing more than involve him in further murders and make it that much more difficult to clear his name. Nevertheless there was only one way he was going to clear his name and that was to find Jonathan Crossland before his sister did, which in turn meant convincing the sheriff that he did not murder Lester Davidson.

'I guess I wasn't thinkin' straight,' said Brogan. 'I'm a stranger in town, as you know, an' I figured gettin' involved would only make trouble for myself. Most sheriff's seem only too ready to make trouble for drifters like me. You just said yourself that you ain't never met a decent saddle bum yet.'

'An' you're no different to any of the others', sneered the sheriff. 'Well you *are* involved and you *are* in trouble.' He grinned broadly. 'I reckon I got me enough evidence to have you up before the judge. In fact I think we might just have enough evidence to have us a hangin' party pretty soon. The judge don't like saddle bums either.'

'You don't have any proof,' protested Brogan. 'Not real proof anyhow.'

'Lawyer are you?' said the sheriff, with a dry laugh. 'You sure seem to be able to talk. I've seen more'n one man sent to the gallows on far less evidence.' He looked Brogan up and down and smiled, shaking his head as he did so. 'I'm a fair man though,' he continued. 'Like you say some sheriffs wouldn't bother. They'd have somebody to blame for a murder an' that'd be good enough. No, Mr . . . What did you say your name was?'

'McNally, Brogan McNally,' said Brogan.

'Right,' nodded the sheriff. 'No, Mr Brogan McNally, I don't believe you murdered Lester Davidson. Sure, we got a very reliable witness who saw you goin' down that alley but she also saw two other men go down just before you did, pushin' another man and then she heard them beatin' somebody. Presumably this other man. That was before she saw you. I reckon you saw 'em as well, maybe you even know their names. Who are they?'

'I can identify 'em,' confirmed Brogan. 'Don't know their names though. I can even take you along to the saloon they seem to use.'

'You know,' said the sheriff, placing the tips of his fingers together and then against his lips as he rested on his elbows. 'I got me this feelin' that there's a lot more to all this than meets the eye.

You strike me as somethin' of a rarity among saddle bums, one who can talk, can probably read an' write and don't seem too scared. Yes, there's a lot more to all this. For instance, why should a saddle tramp be so interested in followin' a boy round town. Don't deny it, my deputy here saw you an' he swears you was followin' a boy. Now why should you do that? I heard about some men who like to do things to boys rather than women or girls but I don't reckon you is one of them. It also seems you was outside the lumber yard askin' some other boys about a fifteen-year-old by the name of Jonathan Crossland or somethin' like that. One of those boys knows my own son and told him so don't deny it. Crossland! Now that's a name I've not heard for a long time an' it might not be the same one. There's a Sam Crossland lives out at Driftwood. I ain't seen or heard from him for years now but I hear he has three boys an' a daughter. I also hear he's done pretty well for himself supplyin' the army with food and horses. I don't suppose it's the same Crossland, one of Sam Crossland's boys?'

Brogan realized that there was little point in denying anything, and he usually found it rather difficult to lie convincingly. He nodded, pulled up a chair and sat opposite the sheriff.

'It's the same Crossland,' he admitted. 'Only thing is, him and two of his boys have been murdered and his daughter, Betty, is tryin' to blame me for it.'

'And did you?' asked the sheriff.

'No, sir, I did not,' said Brogan.

The sheriff nodded.

'No, I don't reckon you did. Now don't you think it'd be a good idea to tell me exactly what's been goin' on? The murders of Sam Crossland and his boys are out of my territory but I might be able to help.'

Brogan nodded and explained what had happened from the first moment he rode into Driftwood.

'OK,' said the sheriff, 'that wasn't too difficult was it? You could be lyin' through your teeth I suppose, but somethin' tells me you ain't. So this Betty Crossland is stayin' at the Metropole Hotel. I might check her out myself. In the meantime I want you to go with my deputy here an' show him just where those two men and the boy are. I'll get some of my other deputies to ask about for this Jonathan Crossland.'

'What about the marshal?' asked Brogan. 'I reckon that by now he's been told about me. I saw her go in his office.'

'Leave him to me,' said the sheriff. 'Just one thing. Don't go doin' anythin' stupid like makin' a run for it. Innocent men don't run.'

6

Brogan led the deputy to the saloon where he had seen the two men and he was not too surprised when there was no sign of them. Whilst the bartender grudgingly admitted to the deputy that they could well be regular customers, he claimed that he had not seen them that day. He pointed out that he was only the bartender and not the saloon-owner and had not arrived for duty until shortly before Brogan and the deputy had arrived.

Brogan then led the deputy to the tumbledown shack where the sneering youth apparently lived. This time they were in luck even though the youth — along with four other youths — attempted to make a break for it as soon as they saw the deputy.

The accommodation seemed to consist of one large, main room around the sides of which about twenty men and boys slept on little more than straw. There was a small, wood-burning stove in the centre of the room, a long, rickety-looking table and two rough benches.

It appeared that the presence of the law was enough to frighten most residents as they tried to avoid looking at them and some seemed to be trying to hide things. The deputy smiled but did nothing. It was Brogan who actually caught the youth as he tried to escape through a loose board in the wall. Somehow he had been fully expecting him to attempt an escape. The youth was then roughly manhandled, protesting loudly, back to the sheriff's office.

It did not take too long for the sheriff to establish that the youth was named Carl Bremner and that he was more commonly known as *Dipper* because of his ability to pick pockets. It was also established that the older of the two men was his uncle, Jimmy Bremner, also known as *Greasy* because of his knack of being able to get into seemingly impossible small and tight places. Greasy was his father's brother and he, Dipper, had moved out West — apparently against his will — to live with his uncle about seven years previously.

He was originally from New York and it had been here, as a small boy, that Dipper had developed his ability to pick pockets and even complicated locks. Inevitably, even as a small boy he had always been in trouble with the law. In fact things had become so bad that his parents had thought it best for him to move out West to live with his uncle mainly, according to Dipper, because they were unable to control him.

'I reckon I'd've been better off stayin' in New York,' complained the youth. 'At least there was always somethin' to do, somewhere to go an' plenty of friends to do it with. Out here there ain't nothin'. Not only that, my pa never made me go out stealin' for him like Uncle Greasy does. I knows I make my livin' stealin' from folk but at least I used to steal for myself. Out here my uncle picks a store or house or somethin' an' I have to go in an' steal what I can. Sometimes he steals things to order, or rather *I* steal to order.'

'You don't have to steal anythin',' Brogan pointed out.

'I tried that,' said Dipper. 'All I got was a good beatin' from my uncle. It was easier to do what they told me to do. I'm seriously thinkin' of headin' back to New York. Only problem with that is gettin' enough money together.'

'Maybe so,' agreed the sheriff. 'Right now though we're not the slightest bit interested in why you're here in Sulphur Springs or what you do, but I'll remember what you've just said. What we want to know is where your uncle and the other man are right now. You do know that Lester Davidson is dead don't you? We think he was murdered by that uncle of yours.'

'Naw,' replied Dipper, almost laughing. 'He don't do things like that, 'specially cuttin' a man's throat. Sure, I knows Lester was murdered an' how. Who the hell don't by now? I don't reckon it was Uncle Greasy though. He might shoot somebody an' more'n like has. Even then he wouldn't stand too close on account of the blood. Shootin' like that wouldn't bother him too much but I don't think he could ever slit a man's throat. That'd be far too much blood for Uncle Greasy. Even the sight of blood usually makes him feel sick. I wish I could've seen his face when Lester's throat was slit. I'll bet he was as sick as a pig. I heard Lester'd been killed just after it happened. News like that travels pretty damned fast, almost as soon as it's happened sometimes an' even when you think nobody saw nothin'. Naw, if either of them did it, it must've been Tex. Blood don't bother him just so long as it ain't his. He's a real mean bastard.'

'Tex?' queried Brogan. 'Tex who?'

'Ain't got the faintest idea,' said Dipper. 'He was around with my uncle when I got here an' he's been here ever since. I ain't never heard nobody call him anythin' but Tex. All I know is he's from Texas. I guess that's why they call him Tex.' He laughed. 'Some folks have very original names, don't they?'

'So where are they now?' demanded the sheriff. 'More important, where is Jonathan Crossland?'

'Johnny's gone an' done a run for it,' said Dipper with a laugh. 'Can't say as I blame him for that either, I would too if somebody was tryin' to kill me. Seems lots of folk are very interested in Johnny Crossland, includin' Mr McNally here. I reckon he's told you all about that though an' he probably has a good reason or else he wouldn't be here with you. I think my uncle an' Tex went after him. Seems like somebody is goin' to pay 'em good money if Johnny ends up dead. An' before you ask, no, they never said nothin' to me about it, they never tell me much about anythin' but I overheard 'em talkin' about it.'

'When was this?' asked Brogan.

'When did they go after Jonathan?'

'Today of course,' replied Dipper. 'Johnny didn't make a run for it until today. That was about three hours ago, I reckon. Can't be much more than that. It warn't that long after Lester Davidson was murdered. They told me to find Johnny but they still came round lookin' for him themselves. They seemed to want Johnny real bad. Don't know how much they was bein' paid to kill Johnny but I'd say it must've been well worth it as far as they were concerned. I reckon it must've been a few hundred dollars. Johnny was ahead of them though, he warn't nobody's fool. He seemed to know it was time to get out of Sulphur Springs an' pretty damned fast at that. I think he'd already made his mind up before all this happened. It was almost as if he was expectin' it. I don't know if he knew about Lester Davidson or not or if he even knew Lester. Probably not.'

'Do you know who hired this Tex and your uncle to kill Jonathan?' the sheriff asked.

'Nope,' said Dipper very firmly. 'Like I said, they never told me nothin'. All I know is it only started this mornin' when I told 'em Lester Davidson was lookin' for Johnny an' that they said they was goin' to ask Lester what it was all about. I even told 'em about you as well.' He looked at Brogan. 'I reckon they didn't bother with you 'cos you look like you can handle yourself an' a gun. Mean bastards as they are, neither of 'em is what you might call brave. Shootin' in the back is more their style. They both had an eye for the easy dollar though, that's somethin' what runs in the family, I guess. I know my pa was the same although he was always more careful. They never missed a chance an' they were good at it too. I had nothin' to do with them killin' Lester an' that's the truth.'

'I believe you,' replied the sheriff. 'Which way did they go?'

'Search me,' shrugged Dipper. 'I didn't even see Johnny leave, one of the others told me Johnny packed his things an' left. I hear tell he had a pony stabled somewheres but I don't know where. That's not the kind of thing a kid with any sense goes around tellin' folk about. Just like I knew he had a gun although he pretended he didn't. Most folk'd soon steal the gun and pony from him, sell the pony for meat an' hide an' the gun an' saddle to a dealer. I was thinkin' about stealin' his gun myself, I could've got at least twenty dollars for it, but I never got the chance. Johnny might've been only fifteen but he sure had a lot of sense. He knew what to say an' when to say it an' he could read an' write proper which is more'n most of us can, includin' my uncle an' Tex. Yes, sir, Johnny had only been in town a couple of days or so but he sure seemed to have attracted a hell of a lot of attention. What the hell did he do, murder somebody or rob a bank?'

'Did he ever say who he was running from?' asked the sheriff, ignoring the question. 'Did either your uncle or Jonathan ever mention if whoever hired them was a woman who might be looking for him?'

'No, never. Johnny never even admitted he was runnin',' said Dipper. 'I didn't know him long enough to find out much. I just knew he was runnin' from somethin' or somebody, that's all. I spent years on the streets of New York an' learned about people an' things like that. Folk on the run have a certain look about 'em. It's hard to say exactly what it is but it ain't often I'm wrong. I know he had some money, don't know how much, but he always seemed to be able to put his hand on a couple of dollars when he needed it. I'll admit, I was lookin' to steal it an' I was workin' on it but I never had the chance to work out where he kept it, but I would've done.

'Then all this happened. I think he had his pony in a livery stable so he must've had some money. Liveries round here always demand payment in advance. Too many folk stop by an' ride on without payin' if they can. Maybe he kept his money there, I don't know but he didn't carry it around with him that's for sure. Don't know where the livery was either but I think it was one on this side of town.'

The sheriff nodded. He called two deputies over and told them to check on every livery stable on the north and east side of town. Dipper was allowed to leave with the warning that since they now knew about him and his activities, the deputies would be keeping a watchful eye on him.

'I sure as hell don't know if it'll do any good,' admitted the sheriff when Dipper had gone, 'but we have to start somewhere and it just might frighten him off, but I doubt it. He's young enough to change but I can see that boy spending a good deal of his time in my cells. As for Jonathan Crossland, even if we do find him I ain't so sure as there's anythin' I can do about him even if he is only fifteen. So far he ain't done nothin' wrong an' as far as I know nobody has tried to kill him up to now. Right now findin' the other two is more important an' I think I can prove they murdered Lester Davidson. I've got me a reliable witness, the one who saw you. That apart, I don't like unsolved murders in my town.'

Less than half an hour later one of the deputies returned with the news that a youth matching the description of Jonathan Crossland had indeed paid for stabling at a small livery stable. He had paid two weeks in advance but had apparently returned to claim his animal earlier that day and had ridden out heading north.

'An' that's just about the worst direction he could've chosen,' muttered the sheriff. 'At least it's just about the worst from my point of view. That's wild country up there but more importantly it's Indian country, although they ain't been no real trouble for a few years. It might be nothin' more'n coincidence or he might've known we can't just ride up there without permission from the Department of Indian Affairs an' believe me, they don't give permission too easily.'

'Is it a reservation? asked Brogan.

'Sure is,' said the sheriff. 'Them Indians might not like it all that much but they also know they got certain rights they never had before. If he's up there I don't see how we can get to him. You've got to have a damned good reason to go up there an' I don't think a boy on the run from his sister or anyone else is a good enough reason. I mean, as far as we know he hasn't done anythin' wrong and we can't even prove that his sister murdered her father and her other brothers and is out to kill him. Even if they do let somebody go up, they always send an Indian policeman with them and they can be very awkward to deal with. It can take a few days before they can get hold of a policeman. It's not a lot of use tryin' to

139

work out where anybody would come out of the reservation either. There must be five or six hundred miles of border; a man could leave the reservation almost anywhere.'

'There's always Bremner an' Tex,' Brogan pointed out. 'They're both wanted for murder aren't they? They might give permission to go after them.'

'But we don't know for sure they went that way,' the sheriff pointed out. 'I need positive proof that they murdered Lester Davidson and that they went into the reservation. I don't have any real proof of either except for one witness. Sometimes the Department of Indian Affairs demands more proof than a court would. They say it's to protect the Indians. That's a laugh. Some of the farmers round the reservation reckon it's an open licence to steal their crops an' cattle. They know what to do about cattle-rustlers but they daren't lift a finger against the Indians even when they see them doin' it.'

'But there's nothin' to stop a drifter like me from goin' up there?' asked Brogan. 'I mean, there ain't no wall round the place is there?'

'Well, I guess not,' admitted the sheriff. 'All the roads have sign warnin' folk but I suppose you could always say you can't read an' didn't know about the reservation. That might work with somebody like you but there'd be no excuse for me bein' there without permission.'

'Well, it's too late to start out now,' said Brogan. 'I'll leave at first light. In the meantime it'd help if I knew whether or not Bremner an' Tex also headed there.'

'I'll tell my boys to find out,' promised the sheriff. 'Check with me before you leave in the mornin'. Right now I've got a young lady to see over at the Metropole Hotel.'

★ ★ ★

Brogan was somewhat surprised to find that Sheriff Seaton was up and about even before he was. Most sheriffs were inclined to lie in their beds in the mornings claiming that hardly anything ever happened in the early mornings. The sheriff was able to confirm that Bremner and Tex had also apparently followed Jonathan Crossland into the reservation. They had been seen by a farmer who lived close to the reservation. He had not seen Jonathan.

'Two things,' said the sheriff. 'First, Betty Crossland claimed that she is looking for her brother because she believes that you are out to kill him. She claims that you murdered her father and her other brothers. She says that she is trying to protect Jonathan. She admits to hiring Greasy Bremner and Tex and even Lester Davidson but says they were only being paid to find him for her. She says she didn't even know Lester had been murdered but that she wouldn't be surprised if it wasn't you who'd killed him.'

'I would have expected nothin' else,' said Brogan. 'On the face of it what could be more natural than for a woman to be worried about her younger brother. What was the second thing?'

'Last night, just after you'd left here, I had me a visit from Marshal James Simpson.' said the sheriff. 'He's looking for you. He's got your name an' a pretty good description. Seems that he had a long talk with Betty Crossland and he seems to believe her story. He insists that you are guilty and therefore wanted for the murders of the Crosslands back in Driftwood. There's nothin' I can do about it either. That's his territory out there not mine. As far as I know he has no idea that I know you or that we've been talking. I know I certainly didn't let on that I had even heard of you an' my deputies wouldn't say a thing without checking with me first. There's no love lost between my office and Marshal Simpson. I had to promise that I'd keep an eye open for you though.'

'Which means that I'd better get the hell out of here pretty damned quick,' said Brogan. 'Does he know about Bremner and Tex?'

'He never mentioned them and neither did I,' said the sheriff. 'I didn't want to let on that I probably knew more than he did.'

'So you don't believe that I had anythin' to do with the Crossland murders?' asked Brogan.

'Maybe I'm too trustin' an' you might stink worse than a skunk,' said the sheriff with a broad grin, 'but no, I don't. Now I suggest you get the hell out of Sulphur Springs right now. If Simpson finds out I do know you he could make life very difficult for me.'

'I'm on my way,' said Brogan. 'Thanks for all your help, Sheriff. If I can, I'll bring Bremner and Tex back for you but I ain't makin' no promises. I need Jonathan to prove I didn't murder his father and brothers.'

'Understood,' said the sheriff with a nod. 'Best of luck an' don't go upsettin' the Indians too much.'

Brogan's tracking skills probably placed him amongst the best trackers in all the states and territories and even beyond. These skills along with his very astute hearing, keen eyesight and even strong sense of smell had developed over a great many years and his very existence had depended on them on many occasions. In addition he seemed to have an inbuilt sixth sense which warned of danger even when there were no obvious signs.

However, it was soon very plain that unless someone had written a sign saying *Jonathan Crossland went that way*, there were far too many recent tracks and many well-used side roads to help much. He kept on heading north. It was not until he came across a broken sign at a crossroads about three hours after leaving Sulphur Springs that the situation improved.

The sign, as expected, informed travellers that to continue heading north meant that they were about to enter the Indian reservation, and that unless they had permission from the Department of Indian Affairs, further progress was forbidden. From that point onwards the tracks became fewer and more readable. Most other tracks had turned either east or west at the crossroads.

After a fairly short time the recent signs revealed three sets of tracks. In some cases two of the sets overlaid the other which soon identified which set belonged to Jonathan and which two sets to Bremner and Tex. The set belonging to Jonathan's pony were slightly smaller than the other two. Brogan also noted that one of the sets belonging to Bremner and Tex showed signs of a defective horseshoe.

At midday Brogan came across a small creek and the fairly recent remains of a camp-fire. The signs were that it had been Bremner and Tex who had stopped. He too rested his horse for a while and during that time discovered the tracks left by Jonathan. He also noted, with a certain amount of concern, that other tracks, this time footprints left by rough shoes, appeared to be following Jonathan. He could only assume that it was one of the Indians. What this represented in terms of danger to Jonathan, Brogan could not be certain.

Since this was a reservation and the Indians were apparently fairly peaceable, it was more than likely that no real harm would come to the boy. On the other hand he had come across cases where the Indians so hated their conditions and the people who forced them to live there that they killed any white man who strayed on to their lands. He could only hope that these Indians were not violently inclined.

However, the discovery had the effect of reminding Brogan that he too was in Indian territory and he immediately began to look round just in case he was also under observation. It appeared that for the moment he was not.

Some time later, he came to the conclusion that Jonathan was making good and rapid progress. In fact he judged from the state of the tracks that the boy was increasing his lead over Bremner and Tex. However, it also appeared that he was now being followed by at least two Indians, now apparently on horseback.

That night, still not having encountered any Indians, Brogan camped alongside a small creek part way up a small hill and the night passed without any incident. However, the following morning he became aware that there appeared to be somebody following him. Whether they were following him by design or accident he could not tell. He could not actually make out who it was, but there was most definitely somebody. He was also eventually able to estimate that there were at least four of them.

That number probably meant that they were Indians and it was always possible that they were not actually following him but just heading in the same general direction. He rode to the top of another slightly higher hill from where he could see all round. He very carefully covered his tracks as he did so, just in case they were following him, and waited for them to come into view.

He had been right, there were four of them and three of them were plainly Indians. The fourth, however, was most definitely not. He was a white man and it most certainly was not Jonathan Crossland.

The group passed below Brogan, no more than a hundred yards away and, seeing the sudden flash of a metal badge on the chest of the white man, he realized that it must be US Marshal James Simpson. The three Indians wore a sort of cavalry-type uniform which, he had to assume, was the uniform of the Indian Reservation Police. It appeared that Marshal Simpson had had no difficulty in obtaining permission to enter the reservation. He also had to assume that the marshal was primarily looking for him and not for Jonathan Crossland.

Brogan allowed the group to get well out of sight before he moved. While he waited Brogan's keen vision also picked out a small dust cloud about five miles ahead. The more he studied the dust cloud, the more convinced he became that there were two riders. Something also told him that they were not Indians, although at that distance it was almost impossible to be certain. He assumed them to be Bremner and Tex. The crucial point was, as far as he was concerned, that the marshal was heading north-east and Bremner and Tex were headed north-west.

It was always possible that Bremner and Tex had no idea where they were or in which direction they were headed and that they had lost Jonathan's tracks. Whatever the reason, Brogan decided to follow Bremner and Tex.

Brogan soon picked up where the two riders had camped for the night and the signs showed that one of the horses had a defective shoe. He now knew that he was definitely following Bremner and Tex. Luck appeared to be on his side as well. Shortly after leaving where Bremner and Tex had camped, he came across the tracks left by Jonathan's pony. It also seemed that Jonathan was still being followed by the two Indians. It was even possible that they were now travelling together.

For the moment Brogan did not want to alarm Bremner and Tex. He was quite confident of being able to deal with them should the need arise. Of rather more concern was whether or not the marshal and the Indian police had eventually picked up on his and the other trails. On several occasions he rode to the top of hills or ridges and looked back. He could see nothing but once again his senses told him otherwise. His suspicions were eventually confirmed when, from the top of a particularly high ridge, he had a clear view of the three Indians and the marshal far below.

For the first time, Brogan felt trapped. In front of him were two men who would not hesitate to kill him, a boy who might shoot first rather than ask questions and two Indians whose reactions could, to say the least, be unpredictable. Behind him was the law, a law which was apparently quite convinced that he had murdered the Crosslands.

7

Brogan was well aware of his abilities, even arrogantly so at times, he knew from years of experience that he could outwit and outshoot almost any man or even groups of men in most circumstances; he knew he could live off the land, find food in even the harshest of deserts and generally survive in ways that most other men would find impossible.

However, despite all this and despite his self-admitted arrogance on these things, he also knew that a good Indian tracker was more than his equal. For perhaps the first time since learning of the murders of the Crosslands, it suddenly really came home to him just how much his life now depended upon his reaching Jonathan Crossland before Bremner and Tex could do so.

He also knew that expecting the law

and Marshal Simpson in particular, to agree with his side of the story would probably be a waste of time. He doubted very much if his version of what had happened to the Crosslands would be believed by Marshal Simpson above that of Betty Crossland.

Betty Crossland had three very important things in her favour: she was family, a woman and apparently without obvious motive. A powerful combination against a dirty, smelly, self-confessed saddle tramp under any circumstances. Brogan also knew that she was a very convincing liar who had apparently already worked her charms upon the marshal. This meant it was vital that the marshal did not capture him before he, Brogan, could reach Jonathan and persuade him to talk. Even Marshal Simpson would be forced to believe Jonathan Crossland.

Brogan knew absolutely nothing about Marshal James Simpson, but in his time he had met enough lawmen of one kind or another to know that many, when convinced of a man's guilt, would shoot him in the back rather than risk their own lives.

Most were also very much in favour of the easier, less time-consuming solution offered by killing a man. There were exceptions: a few genuinely cared about truth and justice. The only problem was that Brogan did not know if Marshal Simpson was one of those exceptions. If Sheriff Seaton of Sulphur Springs was to be believed then it was most unlikely, but the sheriff's dislike of the man could quite easily be attributed to rivalry between the two.

Brogan could not blame any man for not taking unnecessary chances — he liked to think he never did so himself — although shooting a man in the back in cold blood was abhorrent to him. On the odd occasion it had happened to him but he liked to believe that it had always been necessary, never intentional and certainly not cold-blooded murder.

However, he knew that many an innocent man had met his death in such a way. When this happened as far as the law was concerned, the case was closed and the fact that those really guilty were allowed to go free seemed of little importance. A crime had been solved. He had no intention of becoming one of the innocent but dead just to solve a crime.

Nor was he really concerned with Bremner and Tex; they had suddenly become unwanted pieces in the larger picture. They were certainly not now vital to Brogan in his search for Jonathan Crossland other than his reaching Jonathan before they could and that could mean his having to kill them.

However, he still needed to be careful. He did not want to give Marshal Simpson a further excuse to arrest or kill him in the event of his innocence of the Crossland murders being proved. Many lawmen seemed to greatly resent being proved wrong: it apparently hurt their pride and he felt it would make matters worse for no other reason than that he was what he was

— a saddle tramp. Lawmen and saddle tramps very rarely saw eye to eye. If he were to kill either or both of the other men it just might give the marshal the added excuse he needed.

Bremner and Tex might have had some sort of reputation back in Sulphur Springs but as far as he knew they had not actually committed any crimes which could be proved and proving anything against them was certainly not any of his business. That made them innocent men in the eyes of the law and that same law, in the form of Marshal James Simpson, was apparently fully convinced of the guilt of Brogan McNally — *no-good saddle tramp*.

During one of his frequent stops, Brogan climbed to the top of a high, steep ridge and surveyed the land both in front of and behind him.

Behind there was not much vegetation to obscure his view and in the far distance, he could still just make out the marshal and the Indian policemen. They were obviously not in any hurry, simply taking their time and following his tracks. They were plainly experienced enough to know that he was unlikely to escape them. He was not at all surprised that it had not taken them long to realize that they had been heading in the wrong direction earlier.

Ahead of him the nature of the land changed somewhat in that there was much more brush, more stunted thorntrees and fewer cactus plants. At first there was nothing to be seen but eventually his keen eyesight detected movement amongst the dense brush and almost at the limit of his vision.

It was possible that it was a deer but Brogan was experienced enough to think otherwise. He was quite convinced that there were two riders. This seemed to indicate Bremner and Tex. There was absolutely no sign of Jonathan Crossland or the two Indians who might now be with him.

On descending the ridge, he soon discovered tracks which showed that Jonathan and the Indians had headed west. Bremner and Tex had apparently missed the signs and had continued in a northerly direction.

Brogan followed the fresh tracks of Jonathan and the Indians for about fifty yards before dismounting and running back to the point where he had first discovered them. His purpose was quite simple. As well as being a skilled tracker, he also knew how to obliterate his own tracks well enough to fool most men. However, he knew that a really good tracker would not be fooled for too long.

He obliterated them very quickly, satisfied that the Indian policemen would not expect such a thing from a white man and would, he hoped, be fooled for long enough to enable him to reach Jonathan. He knew that they would realize the deception sooner or later, when his tracks were not to be found. He just hoped it would not be sooner.

It soon became obvious to Brogan that the two Indians were now riding *with* and not *following* Jonathan Crossland. The signs also appeared to indicate that Jonathan was travelling willingly with them. At no point had he seen any signs which indicated a struggle or an attempted escape. If there had been a struggle or an attempt to escape then he had missed it, but somehow he did not think so.

The tracks left the relative flat of the plain and made their way up steeper slopes with less brush-covering towards two distant, tall peaks. Brogan was quite certain that they were headed for the gap between the peaks. However, before he could be proved right, darkness descended and he was forced to make camp.

He deliberately chose a sheltered but raised spot from where he had good all-round vision. He knew that it was going to be a long, cold night. Hot days and very cold nights were a feature of this type of country but for his own safety he could not risk lighting a fire and thereby advertise his exact location.

It *had* been a very cold night and it seemed to take longer than usual for the circulation in both himself and his old horse to work properly. He smiled ruefully and was forced to admit that neither he nor his horse were as young as they liked to think they were.

He looked back but this time there was no sign of the marshal or the Indian policemen. However, while it might have delayed them somewhat, he had to assume that his attempt to cover his tracks had not worked. He always assumed the worst scenario, that way he was rarely surprised.

About an hour after starting out, he came across a waterhole and the remains of a fire. It appeared to be about twenty-four hours old and the signs were that it had been Jonathan and his two Indian companions who had spent a night there. They were apparently a day ahead of him. The presence of the fire showed that the

Indians were not concerned about being seen, nor was there any apparent reason why they should be.

The pass between the twin peaks was reached at about midday and quite suddenly, about half-way along, the tracks he had been following were totally obliterated by countless others. It appeared that Jonathan and the two Indians had been joined by other members of the tribe.

This indicated to Brogan that the main Indian settlement was not too far away, although, look as hard as he might, he could see no sign of it. He breathed a little easier. He could hope that his search was almost over. Following so many tracks made his progress that much easier and faster.

★ ★ ★

For a few minutes Brogan's normally very acute senses and self-preservation instincts seemed to desert him and he forgot that life was rarely as simple as it now seemed to be: the bullet painfully skimmed his forehead and thudded into a tree. He deliberately fell from his horse in such a way as to make it appear that he had been hit, which in fact he had been, even if only a scratch. He felt a trickle of blood running down his face.

Feigning death was a ruse he had often used to great effect and one which rarely failed. This time, however, it had been a little too close for comfort, although the blood would add to the realism if necessary. He made certain that his gun was hidden by his body and close to hand should he need to use it.

He had been riding along a small, rock-strewn, narrow valley and the last thing he had expected was an ambush. There was absolutely no reason to assume that such a thing might happen. He doubted if the Indians from the village were responsible, there was no need for them to do such a thing. They would be far more likely to confront him.

That left Bremner and Tex or just possibly Marshal Simpson, both of which possibilities were, in his opinion, most unlikely. The time factor simply did not allow for such a thing unless they had ridden through the night. However, his assailant did not show himself. The only other possibility was a lone, renegade Indian — again most unlikely, or a drifter.

Brogan heard a horse being ridden away and the significance was not lost on him. It had been a lone horse. As such, added to the time factor, that again seemed to rule out Bremner and Tex and the marshal. Added to that was the fact that had it been any of them they would almost certainly have checked to see if he was dead, otherwise there would be little point in trying to kill him.

The fact that it *had* been a lone horse *might* have indicated a drifter but again, simply because they had not checked to see whether he was dead seemed to rule out that possibility.

Nobody was more aware of the more unsavoury habits of his fellow saddle bums than Brogan McNally. Those drifters who killed always did so for purposes of robbery. They would most certainly have looked for something to steal from the body. This one had not.

Having ruled out a drifter on the look-out for easy pickings and dismissed the likelihood of its being Bremner and Tex or even the marshal, that meant that it must have been somebody who knew who he was and who wanted him dead but was also sufficiently inexperienced not to check. Unlikely as it might have seemed, in his mind that left only one person — Betty Crossland.

However, that also meant that Betty Crossland had somehow managed to get in front of him and also meant that she must have a knowledge of the reservation. The chances of her being there by pure chance did not really fit. As to whether or not either she or her brother had any knowledge of the reservation was something he had no way of knowing. But, unlikely as it might have seemed, it was the only thing that made any sense at that moment.

Brogan thought about the direction he had travelled. He realized that in effect he had moved along two sides of a square so it *was* just possible that somebody could have cut along the diagonal and reached the pass before him. The only problem with that theory was that it presupposed that that somebody knew where he was headed and had a good knowledge of the reservation. He did not like the idea very much but at that moment it was all he had.

The fact that his assailant had not checked to see if he was dead appeared to indicate that he or she was very confident in their ability with a rifle or had been fooled by his feigning death.

It had undoubtedly been a rifle shot and he could well imagine that Betty Crossland *was* indeed a very able shot.

She certainly appeared most accomplished in a great many things. It seemed that little more than pure good luck on his part had saved him.

Finding the tracks left by his assailant was not very difficult, even though there were countless other tracks. They were obviously the most recent and were made even more obvious because Indian horses and ponies were not shod. The size of the hoofprints indicated a horse rather than a pony which also seemed to rule out the very slim chance that it had been Jonathan Crossland. However, his luck did not hold out for long, he soon lost the tracks amongst all the others but it did not really matter too much.

From that point onwards he was on full alert and when, after about two miles, the bulk of the tracks turned down a narrow road between two large rocks but he was able to pick up those of his assailant which did not. He was in something of a dilemma.

The tracks made by the Indians

headed down towards a distant river and he was quite certain that the village would not be very far away. Instinct told him that finding Jonathan was his priority but those same instincts wanted to know for certain who it was who had tried to kill him. After a few moments of staring at both sets of tracks he rather reluctantly elected to follow the Indians.

* * *

As he approached the river, Brogan was aware that he was being watched. At first it was nothing more than a sensation he had felt many times before. Initially he could not see anyone but after a short time he saw a lone Indian astride a horse ride to the top of a small rise from where he looked down on him. Brogan raised his hand in acknowledgement but was not too surprised when the Indian simply ignored him. He had little doubt that word he was on the way had already reached the village. He rode on.

About twenty minutes later he was looking down on the mainly skin-covered huts of the village. There were a couple of traditional wigwams but that was all. He looked behind him and was not at all surprised to see four riders now watching him. They made no attempt to come any closer, only moving when he moved.

He studied the village for a few minutes, hoping to see Jonathan Crossland, but there was no sign of him. He felt somewhat apprehensive, looked back at his escort, nodded to them and slowly rode on towards the village. It was not until he was within about thirty yards of the first hut that his escort pulled alongside, two either side. Each had a rifle resting on his thigh which, whilst not immediately threatening, made it very plain that he was outgunned and outnumbered. He grinned at them, nodded and rode on.

An elderly, leathery-faced and weather-beaten figure came out of one of the huts and waited for Brogan to approach him. This was obviously the village headman. Brogan knew better than to dismount without being invited so to do and he also waited for the chief to speak first. He had been taught Indian customs very early on in his life and it had helped him establish a relationship on many an occasion.

'This is reservation land,' intoned the chief. 'You have permission to be here? It is forbidden to enter our territory without permission.'

'I do not have permission,' admitted Brogan. 'I have been following a white boy and I know he came here.'

'A white boy?' grunted the old man. 'How do you know he is here?'

'I have followed his tracks all the way from Sulphur Springs,' said Brogan. 'He came into your village yesterday or possibly this morning along with two of your warriors.'

The old man smiled. 'Warriors!' he said wryly. 'We no longer have need of warriors. The white man's army protects us from our enemies now, although in truth the only enemies we need protection from is the white man and his army. If this white boy *is* here, what do you want with him?'

'I need him to tell Marshal Simpson that I did not murder his father and brothers,' said Brogan. 'Even now the marshal comes for me. Only the boy can prove my innocence.'

'Marshal Simpson comes here for you?' asked the chief.

'He is with three of your Indian policemen,' said Brogan.

Once again the chief smiled wryly and looked at several other elderly men who were listening. He said something to them in their own language and they laughed and nodded.

'The boy is here,' he said. 'We know that he runs from someone who would kill him. How do we know that you do not wish to kill him?'

'Ask him,' suggested Brogan.

'Hand over your guns,' ordered

another man. 'They will be returned to you when the boy confirms what you say.' Brogan handed over his Colt, his Winchester and a knife. 'You may wait for him in that hut,' continued the man. 'He will come to you.'

Brogan was ushered into the hut, the inside of which was very dark and had a slightly sweet and sickly smell about it. One of his guards indicated that he should sit on a hide in the centre of the floor. After what seemed an inordinately long time a slim figure dressed in ill-fitting shirt and jeans appeared, silhouetted against the doorway.

'Jonathan Crossland?' queried Brogan. 'Are you Jonathan Crossland? It's dark in here an' I can't tell properly.'

'My name is Jonathan Crossland,' the boy admitted. 'I saw you arrive. You're that saddle bum, Brogan McNally. I saw you in Driftwood. I saw you in Sulphur Springs as well. Why are you following me?'

'Because my life depends on you telling Marshal Simpson who really murdered your pa an' brothers,' said Brogan.

'He thinks you murdered 'em?' said Jonathan with a dry laugh. 'Yeah, that makes sense. She'd want somebody to lay the blame on an' a saddle tramp would be perfect. Nobody has much time for saddle bums.'

'Ain't nobody knows that better'n me,' said Brogan. 'It was your sister who killed 'em then? I was pretty certain of it but it was just possible I might be wrong. All I know for certain is that it warn't me.'

'And you want me to get you off the hook?' said Jonathan. 'I hear the marshal an' three policemen are headed this way. They're followin' you by all accounts. Why the hell should I help you, Mr McNally? I never did like folk like you an' I didn't like the way you treated me an' my brothers when you rode into Driftwood. It sure don't matter none to me if you're hanged for the murders. I could see you hanged an' then I could come forward an' put the finger on Betty. Ain't nobody goin' to lose no sleep just 'cos an innocent saddle bum was hanged by mistake.'

'That, unfortunately, is very true,' admitted Brogan. 'Did you know that your sister hired two men to find and kill you? Right now they're out there somewhere. They seem to be lost but they could still find you.'

'It figures,' said Jonathan. 'Only way they is goin' to get paid though is when she either kills 'em herself or hands 'em over to the law. Personally I reckon she'll kill 'em an' have a perfectly reasonable explanation all worked out. She's good at makin' folk believe what she says.'

'You obviously know your sister,' said Brogan. 'I personally don't think you've got too much to worry about from them two though. I reckon your sister is your biggest worry. Right now she's also up there somewhere. In fact I reckon she's probably watchin' this village right now.'

'How do you know?' demanded

Jonathan, plainly alarmed.

'See this?' said Brogan pointing to the graze on his forehead. Jonathan peered at it and nodded. 'A rifle bullet did that not too long ago an' that rifle was fired by that sister of yours. It's pure good luck she didn't kill me.'

'I'd say you was right about that,' nodded Jonathan. 'Betty is the best shot with a rifle I've ever seen or ever likely to see.'

'She can't be that good,' said Brogan, boastfully. 'She missed. *I* never miss. Anyhow, she's up there somewhere right now just waitin' her chance to kill you.'

'Then I'm safe as long as I stay here,' said Jonathan.

'Then let's both wait here for the marshal,' suggested Brogan. 'You can tell him what really happened, he can go after her, you can go home an' I can get the hell out of it.'

'No deal, Mr McNally,' said Jonathan. 'Sure, it was Betty who killed Jamie an' Nathan but she didn't kill my pa. That was me an' she saw me do it.'

'*You* murdered your pa!' exclaimed Brogan.

'Single shot, clean through his head,' said Jonathan. 'He found me stealin' his hoard of cash. Three thousand dollars or more. I ain't had a chance to count it all yet an' it don't really matter. He always said there was at least three thousand in that box. Anyhow, Betty came in just as I shot him, Jamie an' Nathan heard the shot, came runnin' an' suddenly Betty grabbed the gun off me an' shot 'em. Next thing I knew she was tryin' to shoot me but the gun must've jammed or somethin'. I never did work out just why she did that. Anyhow, I'd had it all planned, stealin' the money that is. My pony was waitin', I had a bag packed, so while I had the chance before she could kill me, I grabbed the money an' made a run for it. Now it looks like things are workin' out pretty well for both of us. You take the blame for the murders.'

'I'll tell you why she did it,' said

Brogan. 'She wanted the ranch and the only way she could get it legally was to kill her brothers first. The thing is, as I see it, the ranch now belongs to you. If you are out of the way it goes to her. Why did you steal that money and shoot your pa?'

'Shootin' Pa was somethin' I hadn't planned on,' admitted Jonathan. 'As things stood there was no way I was ever goin' to get my hands on the ranch, I never expected to. I didn't want it either an' I sure didn't intend to work on it for the rest of my life. All I wanted was the money so's I could get the hell out of it an' lead my own life. Anyhow, I think you're wrong about the ranch now belongin' to me. I don't think a man who's killed his pa can legally inherit.'

'Then why did she have to involve me?' asked Brogan. 'Why did she have to try to blame me for the murders? All she had to do was tell them you did it.'

'I guess she couldn't take the chance on a jury believin' her story that I murdered all three of 'em once I'd made a run for it an' then got caught,' said Jonathan. 'Either that or she just wasn't thinkin' straight. I reckon she would've claimed that's what happened if that gun hadn't jammed though. She'd've killed an' then claimed it was self-defence or somethin'. Didn't happen that way though, so she blames you knowin' that you have to find me to prove you didn't do it an' hopes that you'll lead her to me. Either way, I guess it don't matter.'

'Yeah,' said Brogan, rather ruefully. 'I always had me this feelin' she was usin' me in some way. I could never figure it out but it makes sense now.'

'That's Betty all right,' said Jonathan with a laugh. 'She always used everybody whenever it suited her an' most times they never realized it.'

8

The confession by Jonathan that he had killed his father had taken Brogan by complete surprise and he was not a man to be surprised that easily. He studied the floor for a few moments before eventually looking up at the boy.

'OK, so the marshal finds us both here,' he said. 'What do you tell him? More important, how do you deal with your sister?'

Jonathan laughed. 'I'm sure me an' Betty can come to some arrangement. Thing is, she wants the ranch an' I don't want anythin' to do with it. That's a good startin' point I reckon. If, like you say, I now legally own it, there ain't no reason to stop me sellin' the place on to her, is there? As for the marshal, he'll only know what Betty saw fit to tell him. I don't suppose Betty has been stupid enough to tell him what really happened. She's probably convinced him that it was you. She's good at things like that. I hear tell the marshal is out lookin' for you so he must think you did it. No, Mr McNally, I don't reckon there's no problem. The marshal arrests you: you hang: me an' Betty do a deal on the ranch an' we both get what we want. You can tell the marshal what the hell you like, he ain't goin' to believe you an' neither is no jury. Nobody ever believes a dirty old saddle bum.'

'How old did you say you was?' asked Brogan. 'You sure don't sound like no fifteen-year-old I ever met before.'

'I grew up fast,' said Jonathan.

'It seems like you've got it all fixed up,' said Brogan. 'It also seems like you an' these Indians know each other pretty well. How come?'

'The old man — the chief — and a few of the others worked for my pa before they got the reservation,' said Jonathan. 'I know Pa had a lot of respect for the Indians an' I hear tell he treated 'em pretty good. Leastways none of 'em have a bad word for him. Sometimes, even now, some of the others come to the ranch for a few months' work. I was all for ridin' right on through the reservation, it's the straightest way north but the two who found me managed to persuade me to come here. I'm glad I did now, things are turnin' out better'n I expected.'

'So Betty bein' up here ain't no real surprise,' said Brogan. 'She must know most of 'em as well. I expect she met up with some of 'em an' they told her where the village was.'

'Somethin' like that,' said Jonathan with a laugh. 'There was a few of 'em in Sulphur Springs. They probably told her. Thing is, Mr McNally, whatever happens to me or her, it looks like it's you what's goin' to hang for the murders, an' you know what? I couldn't give a damn.'

'They've got to catch me first,' said Brogan, standing up.

'You'll be handed over to 'em by the chief just to show that he's a good, law-abidin' reservation Indian,' said Jonathan. Brogan was suddenly aware that Jonathan had a gun aimed at him. 'Don't even think about tryin' to escape, Mr McNally,' continued Jonathan. 'I ain't never killed nobody before except my pa, an' to be perfectly honest I didn't find that difficult at all. In fact it gave me quite a good feelin'. I reckon if I felt good about shootin' my own pa I sure won't have no problem shootin' you. I'd much rather hand you over alive though. That way my an' Betty's story will be all the more believable in court. Whatever you say will be seen as just a dirty old saddle bum lyin' like hell to save his own skin. Killin' you could make things just that bit more difficult, although I'd probably get away with self-defence. You can tell whatever story you like, nobody ain't goin' to believe you. In fact the more you insist it was me an' her the more you'll convince a jury we didn't do it I reckon.'

'And when will you tell your sister about what you've decided to do?' asked Brogan. 'And how do you know it'll be the same story as she's already told the marshal? She was out to kill you, I'm pretty damned sure of that. I reckon you know it too.'

'What's to tell?' said Jonathan with a wry laugh. 'Anyhow, you've just told me what she said happened. I just tell the marshal you came here to kill me 'cos I managed to escape when you killed my pa an' brothers an' I could identify you. As for why Betty is up here? Sure, I know as well as you that she came to kill me but as far as the marshal is concerned, ain't it only natural for an older sister to be worried about her kid brother? More especially so when somebody like you is out to kill him? She'd know why I came to the reservation, they're my friends. Betty sure ain't stupid. She wouldn't dare kill me while the Indians are around. It won't take her more a couple of seconds to catch on to what's goin' on either. She sure as hell ain't dumb so I reckon she'll agree to what I say.'

'You're forgettin' about the other two, Greasy Bremner an' Tex,' reminded Brogan. 'Just like you're forgettin' about the money you stole. How do you explain that?'

'Another two no-good layabouts, just like you,' said Jonathan. 'I saw 'em back in Sulphur Springs. Greasy Bremner was Dipper Bremner's uncle. And the money? That's easy to explain. That was the reason you murdered Pa an' my brothers. Three thousand dollars must be a hell of a lot of money to a man like you. You tried to rob Pa, things went wrong, you had to shoot him an' my brothers. Somehow though — I ain't even sure myself how 'cos it all happened so sudden — I grabbed the money off you an' made a run for it. Yeah, a jury would like that, not bein' able to say exactly what happened. All they'll see is a fifteen-year-old boy who's had the hell scared out of him. Thing is, if you're right an' I do own the ranch, that money now belongs to me anyhow.'

Brogan sighed, shook his head and smiled to himself. Even he had to admit that at that precise moment it appeared that the normally invincible Brogan McNally had been outwitted by a woman and a fifteen-year-old boy. The time-factor argument he had used when first confronted by Luke Briscoe would probably be completely ignored in the unlikely event that he was ever brought before a court. He believed somebody would try to kill him before that was allowed to happen.

It was also very obvious that Jonathan Crossland was not going to give Brogan the opportunity to over-power him. As Brogan moved, so Jonathan also moved closer to the doorway. He suddenly called out and three young Indians burst in, each pointing rifles at Brogan. Brogan simply shrugged, once again allowed himself a wry smile, and raised his hands slightly in a gesture of submission. Nevertheless one of them rammed his rifle into Brogan's belly and grinned.

One of them spoke to Jonathan in the Indian language and Jonathan replied. It was plain that Jonathan was very fluent as quite a long conversation took place. Eventually Jonathan smiled at Brogan.

'They tell me the marshal is almost here,' said Jonathan. 'You'll be kept in here until he does get here and there'll be at least three guns aimed at this hut all round until then.' Jonathan ducked through the low doorway, pausing to look back. 'Thanks for all your help, Mr McNally, I'll make sure you get a decent burial. It's the least I can do.'

When he was alone, Brogan lifted the corner of a hide covering the frame of the hut and saw four young men standing facing the hut, each with a rifle in hand at the ready. He did the same in two other places and counted at least eight more men with rifles. Had it been dark he might have attempted an escape but he dismissed the idea as impossible at that moment.

Quite apart from not having any

weapons and not knowing where his horse was, Brogan McNally liked to believe that he never took unnecessary risks, even on the odd occasion his life had been in imminent danger. His usual thinking was that at least he was still alive and would look to take his chance if and when one presented itself. He was always somewhat surprised that these opportunities did suddenly appear, usually because of human error on the part of his captors and he was always ready to take advantage.

Marshal James Simpson and the three Indian policemen arrived about half an hour later and at first there was a lot of talking which Brogan could not hear properly. He had no doubt that the marshal was being made aware of all the *facts* as Jonathan thought they ought to be. Eventually Brogan was ordered out of the hut to face the marshal.

'I guess this is the end of the road for you,' said the marshal. 'Young Jonathan has told me what happened an' it's more or less the same as his sister told me. I'm takin' you back to Driftwood where you'll be put on trial.'

'If I ever get there,' said Brogan.

'If you ever get that far,' agreed the marshal, nodding his head sagely. 'I've had outlaws try to escape before now an' they've all ended up dead. Saves a whole lot of bother too. You're welcome to try it any time you like. Anyhow, it's too late to think about gettin' back to Sulphur Springs now, but don't you go thinkin' it gives you the chance to escape. There'll be guns all round this hut all night an' just to be doubly sure, your hands an' feet will be tied.'

'I thought you wanted me to try and escape,' said Brogan.

'Better if there's no witnesses,' replied the marshal with a broad grin.

The Indian policeman who tied Brogan's wrists and ankles used thin leather thongs and made a very good job of it and Brogan, try as he might, could not get out of his bonds. After a couple of hours he gave up even trying.

*   *   *

'What about the two men Betty Crossland hired to find her brother?' asked Brogan when the marshal came to see him the next morning. 'I know she hired them to kill the boy.'

'Do you now?' asked the marshal with a broad grin. 'She told me about them, told me she'd only hired them to find the boy but she seemed to think they'd got the wrong idea an' were out to kill him. She says she was told that by somebody who knew Bremner back in Sulphur Springs. She made a point of tellin' me about it the moment she found out. That don't sound like a woman out to murder her own family to me. I don't know where Bremner an' this Tex feller are at this moment an' I don't really care. If I find 'em I'll take 'em in, if I don't they'll get caught sooner or later, folk like that always do.

189

I'll send out some scouts to find 'em. They've got nowhere to run.'

Brogan was forced to laugh, which rather surprised the marshal.

'Hell, that woman has it all worked out don't she?' said Brogan. 'If Jonathan is killed by them two she only has to remind you that she warned you about it. She still gets what she wants though. If they don't kill him then she falls in line with what her brother says an' she still gets what she wants — the ranch.'

'Yeah, Jonathan said you'd say somethin' like that,' said the marshal. 'Accordin' to him you reckon *he* killed his father and that his brothers were killed by his sister an' they aim to split what's left between them. He takes the money and she gets the ranch. Nice try, McNally, but I don't think it's goin' to work. If they was in it together there'd be no reason for him to run. No jury is ever goin' to believe you against them.'

'That's what I'm constantly bein' told,' said Brogan. 'It probably won't get as far as a court room though. For what it's worth, Marshal,' he continued, 'that's what really did happen except that he was on the run 'cos his sister tried to kill him too. Still, like you say, I don't reckon no jury will ever believe me. I mean, I am only a dirty old saddle bum an' I ain't got no real proof at all.'

'Now you're talkin' my kind of language,' said the marshal with a dry laugh. 'With luck, you'll get your chance to say what you think in court.'

'With luck,' said Brogan with a resigned shrug of his shoulders.

* * *

Surprisingly, the three Indian policemen were not detailed to escort Brogan and the marshal back to Sulphur Springs. Instead one was sent to find Betty Crossland and the other two were dispatched to look for Greasy Bremner and Tex, with the instruction that they were to take absolutely no chances on being killed or injured themselves.

In other words the Indians had permission to shoot on sight which was what they probably would do. Jonathan elected to remain in the Indian village until his sister was found. This was probably because he felt safer amongst the Indians and knew that she would not attempt to kill him whilst they were around.

Brogan was set astride his old horse with his wrists again firmly tied in front of him to allow him to grip the horn of his saddle. The marshal tied a lead rope between his saddle and Brogan's horse. The pair left the village in complete silence. Brogan was tempted to say something to Jonathan as he rode past him but he simply nodded and smiled. Jonathan grinned at him and spat on the ground.

They rode steadily until about midday when the marshal pulled up alongside a small, clear stream. He untied Brogan's hands to allow him to perform certain essential bodily functions and to quench his thirst. Once

Brogan had finished he retied his hands.

During all the time between starting out that morning and stopping, hardly a word had passed between them. Brogan really did not mind, any conversation would have been irrelevant in any case. It also gave Brogan more time to try and work out a plan of escape. With his hands tied as firmly as they were though, opportunities appeared non-existent.

'How long's it goin' to take?' Brogan asked.

'Two days,' replied the marshal. 'I ain't in no hurry.'

'I meant what I said — about Betty Crossland an' Jonathan,' said Brogan. 'It's them who should be on their way back for trial, not me.'

'You'll have your chance to say your piece,' said the marshal. 'I wish I had five dollars for every outlaw who claimed he was innocent. I'd be a very rich man.'

'I guess so,' admitted Brogan. 'That

don't help those who *are* innocent though. Do I have to ride with my hands tied? I ain't got no gun an' I don't reckon this old horse of mine could ever outrun yours. Takes her all her time to put one foot in front of the other most of the time.' His horse pricked up her ears and snorted. 'Understands every word I say though. I wouldn't be without her,' continued Brogan with a broad grin.

'No deal, McNally,' said the marshal with a dry laugh. 'I was caught out like that once, just the once, many years ago. Nearly died that time an' I allus said it would never happen again.'

★ ★ ★

A single shot echoed around the sides of the small, narrow valley and the marshal rolled to the ground, blood quickly soaking his shirt from a wound in his chest. In an instant Brogan had rolled behind a rock where he waited helplessly. To his surprise there were no more shots and nobody came forward to look at their handiwork.

'I knows it's you out there, Miss Betty,' Brogan called. 'Now's your chance to kill me once and for all. You missed the last time.'

'Yes, that *was* a bad shot. I was sure I'd hit your head,' she replied.

'You did,' Brogan called again. 'Just a graze though.'

'In a way it was probably as well,' she called. 'I was going to shoot *you* just now but then I got to thinking. This way you get the blame for murdering the marshal as well as my father and brothers and the law doesn't like it when their own get killed. If I had killed you and not the marshal he would have been forced to accept your story and it could have made life very difficult. Not that it would have been of any interest to you. Killing you both wouldn't have helped much either. That would have made it obvious that somebody else was involved. Oh, I'm sure you've explained everything to Mr Simpson but I don't suppose he believed you. You probably realize by now that I can be very persuasive.'

'I'll say this for you an' your brother,' said Brogan, 'you both seem to know how to work things out. I think Jonathan is ready to do a deal with you. He's admitted to me he murdered your pa but that it was you who murdered your brothers. He says he don't want the ranch. He'll take enough money to make himself comfortable an' you can have the ranch.'

'And if you believe that, Mr McNally,' she called with a loud laugh, 'you'll believe anything. We both want it *all* and I intend to make sure that it is me who gets it. I'll go along with whatever Jonathan says for as long as needs be and he'll go along with me, but believe me either he'll kill me or I'll kill him at the first opportunity. It's easy to arrange accidents. Before that though, you'll be hanged for murdering my father, my brothers and the marshal, leaving us both free to do what we want. I'm normally a pretty good shot, Mr McNally. Is he dead? It's OK, you can check, I'm not going to kill you.'

'Why don't you check yourself?' replied Brogan.

'Because the sight of blood makes me sick,' she said with a laugh. 'It's true, I can't stand the sight of it. I was very ill after killing my brothers.'

'Then you'll just have to assume that he is,' he called.

'I think he is,' she said. 'I hit him in the middle of his chest, I know that and there aren't many who survive a bullet in the heart. I won't offer to untie you, Mr McNally. I'm quite certain that a man like you will soon find a way of freeing himself. Good day to you. I must go and work things out with Jonathan.'

There was silence, although Brogan's keen hearing did pick up the slight sound of a horse being ridden away.

Brogan struggled forward, knelt down beside the body of the marshal and pressed his ear against his face. There was no doubt about it, the marshal was still breathing but there was no way of knowing for how much longer. It could prove very difficult for him if the marshal died.

His priority now was to free himself and to this end he found a knife tucked in the marshal's belt. Having his wrists tied in front made things much easier. He took the knife, laid it on a flat rock with the blade sticking out, held it firm by clamping the handle with his foot and then worked the leather thongs binding his wrists along the blade. In a matter of a couple of minutes he was free.

Then he once again knelt beside the marshal and felt his blood soaked shirt for signs of a heartbeat. The marshal was very plainly still alive and Brogan ripped open the shirt to expose the marshal's chest.

He had seen worse and he had also seen what were apparently lesser wounds from which the man had died. He did not bother to clean up the blood, instead he cut what remained of the shirt off the marshal's body and packed it around the wound in an attempt to staunch the flow of blood. Suddenly the marshal opened his eyes.

'Seems like you were right,' he croaked. 'I heard everythin' she said. I guess that puts you in the clear.'

'It's OK for you to say that now,' replied Brogan, 'but it won't mean a darned thing unless I get you to a doctor pretty damned quick an' you tell somebody else. Don't you go dyin' on me now. I'll strike a bargain with you. I save your life, you save mine. Is it a deal?'

'You got yourself a deal, McNally,' the marshal croaked again.

'You're in a hell of a mess, Marshal,' said Brogan. 'Just gettin' you on your horse could finish you off. I can't risk it. Any idea where the nearest homestead is? If I can get you that far I can ride into Sulphur Springs an' get the doc.'

'The Indians are the nearest,' coughed

the marshal. 'I guess that ain't much use though, not if Jonathan an' Miss Betty are there.'

'No, that would be askin' for trouble,' said Brogan. 'There must be a homestead somewhere's near here.'

The marshal groaned and closed his eyes. Brogan feared the worst. For some time he fully expected the marshal was about to die and there was absolutely nothing Brogan could do about it. It was very plain that any attempt to move the marshal would only make matters worse. The marshal had lapsed into what seemed to be either deep sleep or a coma.

Brogan found his Colt in the marshal's saddlebag and his Winchester strapped to the marshal's saddle. He also found another shirt in the saddlebag. Further examination of the wound showed that the flow of blood had almost stopped, although it was still oozing slightly. The marshal was still breathing, if harshly and with rasping noises coming from his chest but at least he was still alive. All Brogan could do was hope. He ripped the shirt to make rough bandages which he somehow wrapped round the marshal's chest.

Brogan pondered the options now open to him. The simplest was to ride out, leave the marshal and the two Crosslands to sort themselves out in whatever way they chose and for him to take his chance. There were many places where he could probably escape the law for some considerable length of time. However, being the kind of man he was, there were two good reasons as to why he could not take that course.

The first reason was his pride. Never, in almost an entire lifetime of well over fifty years — he did not know exactly how old he was — and all of it from the age of about fourteen spent drifting, had he been a wanted outlaw. He prided himself in never having stolen anything, never having robbed anyone and never having murdered anyone.

True, he had killed many times, but

in his mind at least, there had always been just cause. He did not want to become a outlaw at this stage in his life and have to spend his remaining years looking behind him.

The second reason was the marshal: he simply could not leave the man to die. If at all possible he had to save his life. He laughed to himself. He wondered if anyone else would feel the same about him. He doubted it very much but that did not alter his own feelings.

He also needed the marshal to live simply so that he could clear himself of the charge of murdering the Crosslands and to save him from becoming a fugitive on the run. That last part alone was sufficient to ensure that he must do his best for the marshal.

The marshal remained unconscious for the better part of the remaining daylight hours. He eventually opened his eyes and smiled slightly shortly before nightfall.

'Glad to see you're still here,' croaked

the marshal. 'I thought maybe you'd make a run for it.'

'An' I'm glad to see that *you're* still here,' replied Brogan. 'I could've run out on you but that would've been as good as admittin' I was guilty of them murders. I knows us drifters have a bad reputation, Marshal, but we ain't all bad. Believe me or believe me not, but I ain't never stole nothin' off nobody an' I ain't never murdered nobody. Sure, I've killed me a few who deserved it, but that's all. Now, I asked you a question before you decided to have a sleep. Where's the nearest homestead?'

'Best part of a day's ridin' due west,' croaked the marshal. 'Silas Grant's place. He runs a sheep station on the edge of the reservation. Good man too. His wife knows a thing or two about nursin', fixin' broken bones an' diggin' out bullets. She helped look after wounded soldiers durin' the war.'

'Due west,' mused Brogan. 'That's goin' to take us further away from Sulphur Springs. This woman might be good, but you really need a proper doctor. Somehow I've got to get you to Sulphur Springs.'

'I'll give you odds I don't make it,' said the marshal with a weak grin.

'An' I'll give you odds you do if I have anythin' to do with it.'

9

Brogan was well aware that even the apparently simple act of getting the marshal on to his horse could very easily kill him. Even should he survive that ordeal it was quite possible that the physical effort of riding could finish him off. He needed to be kept as flat and as still as possible. The only thing he could think of was to construct a litter of the type used by the Indians which was dragged behind a horse.

He *had* made these litters before — there were not many such things he had not made or used during his lifetime of drifting. They were simple enough to make and were surprisingly robust and efficient. There were not too many suitable trees about, but he did spot a small clump of likely-looking saplings further down in the small valley.

He explained to the marshal what he intended to do. He nodded but did not really seem to understand and appeared to be drifting off into unconsciousness again. Brogan made certain that he was as warm and as comfortable as possible and went to cut down the saplings.

In the absence of an axe or machete, cutting down meant bending the saplings until they splintered at the base and then using his knife to cut the shattered pieces. That method was all very well for the thinner pieces he needed but the two outer poles, which took all the weight, needed to be of stouter wood. These he eventually made by climbing a tree to cut and break off suitable branches

It was slow but he eventually succeeded and had all the pieces he needed back at the fire — which he had lit some time earlier — just as nightfall closed in. He then set to peeling long, narrow strips of bark. These would be used instead of rope, to bind the saplings and the two stouter poles together. The whole process took rather longer than he had expected but eventually he had completed the litter. He was now feeling very hungry.

There were a few pieces of dried salt pork and some beans in the marshal's saddlebags, along with some ground coffee-beans and some sugar. There was a small stream close by so water was not a problem. He also had a cooking-pot and a billy amongst his own possessions and eventually made himself something edible. He was quite capable of living off the land but it was now too dark to start looking for rabbits, snakes or lizards. He had eaten better pork but he had most certainly tasted worse. Actually he was more grateful for the coffee than the food.

He tried to make the marshal eat, but it was soon plain that he was wasting his time. He did, however, manage to force some hot coffee between the man's lips and this seemed to do some good.

Brogan did not get much sleep that

night; during the day it could be hot enough to scorch a man's skin but in the middle of the night it could become cold enough to freeze that same man to death. There had been many unwary travellers who had perished in this way. Occasionally even their horses had been known to freeze to death. This particular night was completely cloudless and, exposed as they were high up in the mountains, proved much colder than many he had encountered. His one concern was of one or both of them freezing to death.

He pulled the marshal as close to the fire as he dared and even so ensured that he was well wrapped up in both his own and Brogan's blanket. He made certain that there was a good supply of wood and seemed to be constantly checking on the marshal's condition throughout the night.

Not that going without sleep occasionally bothered Brogan all that much. Over the years he had developed the technique of sleeping in the saddle.

Even without that ability he had gone without sleep many times and felt none the worse for it. At least he thought he felt no ill effect but was wise enough to know that advancing years were beginning to make their mark. He often wondered how much longer he could survive the elements in this way, although he always maintained that when his time did come he would want it to be somewhere out in the wilderness.

The night proved long and uneventful and shortly after dawn and after a hot coffee, Brogan laid the marshal on the litter, hitched it to the marshal's horse and started out. The marshal, although still alive, was oblivious to everything that was happening, a state of affairs which suited Brogan. Several times during the morning he checked that he was still alive.

It was about midday when Brogan stopped as a flock of birds suddenly flew up about fifty yards ahead.

They were at the head of a narrow,

wooded valley, in itself no problem at all, but on this occasion, coupled with the sudden flight of the birds, Brogan felt a distinct sense of unease. There could have been many reasons for the birds taking flight and in the normal course of things he might not have taken too much notice. However, the one thing he had learnt in his lifetime and one which had kept him alive on many occasions, was never to ignore his senses or feelings even when there was no obvious reason for such feelings. In fact he had often found that that was just the time to be *more* vigilant.

He left the two horses tethered to a small tree, took his rifle and slowly ventured forward on foot. All the time his senses were on full alert, ready to react to the first sign of danger. His sense of hearing was such that he was normally able to differentiate between what were the natural sounds of the terrain and those which were out of place. He also claimed that he could hear a fly land on a piece of dung from a hundred yards away. This claim was plainly an exaggeration but his hearing was remarkably acute.

In this instance he was quite convinced that he could hear somebody or something breathing or, to be more precise, gasping for breath. It was not too heavy but nevertheless definitely somebody or something breathing. The more he listened the more convinced he became that it was human and not animal. He would have been hard put to explain the difference to anyone but he could tell the difference. He crept forward a few more yards.

The sight that greeted him as he peered down into a small hollow was something he had only ever seen once in his life before and then when he was little more than a youth.

Two naked men were tied, spread-eagled but upright, between trees. The men were in effect taking their full weight on their wrists. Their bodies appeared to have been badly mutilated. There was blood and flies everywhere and already several crows and a solitary buzzard were taking a wary interest in the bodies. It was more than likely that it had been the arrival of the buzzard which had alarmed the other birds. He also had the feeling that the foxes and polecats were not too far away.

Brogan did not do anything immediately. He had long since discovered that rushing in to any situation was, as often as not, a good way to end up in trouble no matter how distressing that situation might be. Instead he listened and looked even more intently.

This was plainly the work of Indians, although it had been many years since he had heard of such barbarity. His caution was for his own sake, not the two men in front of him, whatever he might do would make very little difference to their eventual fate and he had no intention of rushing in and possibly suffering the same fate himself. After a few minutes he was satisfied that there were no Indians around and he slipped into the hollow.

The first man was obviously dead. Brogan pushed his swollen head back and lifted the man's bloodied eyelids to reveal what he had half expected — his eyes had been gouged out. The second man was the man he had heard gasping for breath. Somehow he was still alive although again sightless. Brogan cut them both down and again looked and listened warily. The fact that the blood was barely beginning to congeal more or less confirmed the impression that the incident had happened only a short while previously.

Once again, after a short time, he was reasonably certain that whoever was responsible was not near by.

He cleaned the man's face as best he could and immediately recognized him as Greasy Bremner. It seemed logical to Brogan that the Indian policemen had found them and, taking the marshal at his word, had indulged in an orgy of torture. He did not think there was anything he could do for Greasy, it was simply a matter of when and not if, he

213

would die. He returned to the marshal and the horses and led them to the hollow, where he forced some water into the mouth of the injured man. It really was a futile gesture but one that seemed right at that moment. Greasy gurgled slightly as the water coursed down his throat. He coughed some blood and opened his bloodied mouth.

'Bitch!' he rasped.

'Bitch?' queried Brogan, giving Greasy a little more water.

'Evil bitch,' repeated Greasy. 'She told 'em to do it. Said it was payment for *not* killin' her brother.'

'You mean Betty Crossland is responsible for this?' urged Brogan.

'Can't see,' Greasy moaned and gulped. He was obviously dying. 'Can't see, can't see nothin'. Filthy bitch. She told 'em to torture us. *Have some fun*, that's what she said to 'em. Only way savages know of havin' fun is to torture somebody.'

'Did you actually see her?' Brogan urged again.

214

'I saw her,' rasped Greasy. 'That's more'n I can do now.'

'But she can't stand the sight of blood,' said Brogan. 'It makes her sick.'

'She was with them Indians,' hissed Greasy. 'They found me an' Tex an' she told 'em to *have some fun*. She rode off. Said somethin' about meetin' up with 'em at some place called Rattle-snake Rocks.'

'Rattlesnake Rocks!' said Brogan. 'Any idea where that is?'

'Rattlesnake Rocks,' spluttered Greasy.

His expression suddenly changed, his face muscles became tight as though he was in great pain. His body arched slightly and a long gasp escaped through his now tight lips. Greasy Bremner was dead.

Brogan looked at the still uncon-scious body of Marshal Simpson and nodded. If anyone would know where Rattlesnake Rocks was, he would.

However, finding Rattlesnake Rocks or searching for Betty Crossland were well down Brogan's list of priorities.

Whatever the legal position was regarding the actions of the Indian policemen — and he had no doubts that it was illegal even if it did happen on the reservation — it was nothing at all to do with Brogan and he had no intention of becoming involved. His one concern was to get Marshal James Simpson to Sulphur Springs alive, hand him over to a doctor and hope to clear his own name.

He did not even bother to bury the two men before he continued his journey: he had found that it was almost always a waste of time. Foxes and polecats and even coyotes were very adept at digging up corpses and he had seen the unpleasant result of such diggings on several occasions.

Wolves had apparently been known to eat human corpses — or so it was claimed by some, although somehow he doubted this. Wolves always tried to avoid man, even when there was no other food source and in all his years of drifting he had never seen any evidence

216

of wolves eating a human corpse.

There seemed to be plenty of crows and now another buzzard about who would most definitely feed on a human corpse, as would the countless number of insects, maggots, mice, rats and other small rodents. They would all feed well for a few days or even a couple of weeks. He noted that the men's horses and guns and even trousers and boots were missing and had to assume that they had been taken by the Indian policemen. That made sense, horses, saddles and guns were valuable items and trousers and boots were always useful.

His main concern was that his presence in the area would, if it had not already done so, although he did not really believe that, become known to the Indian policemen or even to Betty Crossland. What the reaction of the Indians would be if they saw the marshal in his present state he could only guess at. The reaction of Betty Crossland would be far more predictable.

He very warily continued his journey through the narrow, thickly wooded valley, stopping frequently to listen and to look at the tree-tops where he could see them. He was prepared for an ambush at any moment. The reactions of birds were always a good indication of any impending danger, as had been the case when he had come across the two bodies.

Neither the Indians nor Betty Crossland had made any attempt to cover their tracks. The Indians were probably not expecting anyone to be following. Even if Betty Crossland might have expected Brogan, she was plainly not at all concerned. Whether she had told the Indian policemen about him he did not know, but there was no attempt to ambush him.

An hour later, he found himself at the end of the valley and looking down on another flat valley, this time quite wide, perhaps two miles across but with a river or rivers meandering across it in numerous tentacles. The whole area was covered in lush, thick brush, a few trees, and countless numbers of large rocks. He looked up and down but there was no alternative other than to cross it. At least there was a reasonable amount of cover should he need it.

Once again, before venturing from the relative safety of the valley, he looked and listened for signs of life, although this time he relied rather more on his keen sight than on sound.

Apart from a small herd of deer about half a mile towards his left and a large bear turning over a rock at the water's edge about 400 yards to his right, there was no sign of anyone. In actual fact the presence of the deer and the bear was a good indication that all was otherwise normal. Even so, he ventured down with great care as the only route down brought him closer to the bear. Bears were the one animal with which Brogan always felt most uncomfortable. He was eventually within about a hundred yards of the animal.

Brogan kept the bear in sight and at

first it seemed not to notice him, but suddenly it reared itself on its hind legs, looked in his direction and sniffed the air. It had caught his scent if not sight of him. For a few moments the bear looked in his direction but then dropped to all fours and moved off in the opposite direction. Brogan breathed a big sigh of relief.

It had been a large animal and bears were, in Brogan's experience, completely unpredictable. Sometimes they would completely ignore a man only a few yards away but on other occasions they would chase after that same man when he was a hundred yards away. They had a very keen sense of smell and sometimes the scent of blood would arouse their interest and the interest of a bear was always unhealthy for anyone. They were also notoriously difficult to kill even with a rifle used by an expert. Brogan had himself emptied his rifle into a bear and not stopped it. A handgun was completely useless.

He had to pick his way through the

numerous streams with great care; he did not want to risk drowning the marshal. Eventually, about an hour later, he was climbing out of the valley and up towards a high ridge. He had no idea what was beyond the ridge.

Reaching the top of the ridge was not too difficult and he had just started down the other side and was heading towards what appeared to be a pass when a shot suddenly rang out. To his surprise the shot did not seem to be aimed at him, in fact it seemed to come from some distance away. However, he pulled the marshal's horse between two large rocks and well off the trail.

He left both horses, took his rifle and ventured forward on foot. Once again a shot rang out and on this occasion he was able to pin-point where it came from. He made his way forward a few more yards before climbing to the top of a large, rocky outcrop.

He peered over just in time to see Jonathan Crossland picking up what appeared to be a dead rabbit. Jonathan held up his prize and called out. Another figure appeared from behind a large rock. Betty Crossland. Brogan moved his position and saw that they seemed to be making camp.

As far as Brogan was concerned this was not a good thing. There was still at least two hours of daylight remaining, valuable hours during which he could get that little bit nearer to Sulphur Springs and a doctor. He looked about for an alternative way through but there did not appear to be one.

Once again he was surrounded by almost sheer cliffs, many up to 150 feet or more and to proceed he had to pass their camp. He also knew that going back would achieve nothing. He had no alternative but to proceed.

He was quite confident of being able to deal with both Betty Crossland and Jonathan if he had to and he was prepared to shoot them if necessary, although that was the last thing he wanted to do. They were, in a sense, his alibi.

He remembered that Greasy Bremner had mentioned Rattlesnake Rocks and that Betty had said she would meet the Indians there. He wondered whether this was Rattlesnake Rocks. If so, it was always possible that the Indians were not too far away. Once again he strained his ears and his eyes.

Eventually he was satisfied that the Indians were not in the vicinity and decided that his best course of action would be simply to ride through and pretend surprise when he saw them. Betty Crossland had said that she wanted to see Brogan hanged for the murders of her family and Marshal Simpson, so it was unlikely that she would attempt to kill him. The only problem with that idea was that the marshal was not dead and that little fact might just change her mind.

He made his way back and looked down on the marshal who was still unconscious. Somehow he had to make it appear that he was dead. He removed the marshal's belt and then wrapped the blankets round the marshal's body and even loosely covered his head. He found a length of twine amongst his own belongings and wound that and the belt round the body. He hoped it was sufficient to make both Betty and Jonathan believe the marshal was dead.

The deception stood a good chance providing the marshal did not choose that moment to recover consciousness. That possibility was something about which Brogan could do absolutely nothing other than be prepared for anything either of them might attempt.

'Well now if it isn't Mr Brogan McNally,' said Betty Crossland, giving Brogan a sarcastic grin as Brogan came into view. 'What the hell have you got there, Mr McNally?'

Both she and her brother barred Brogan's way, their rifles, whilst not aimed at Brogan, held ready. Betty appearing very confident whereas Jonathan was plainly very concerned.

'You ought to know, Miss Betty,' Brogan responded. 'You killed him.

Marshal James Simpson.' He looked at Jonathan and smiled. 'She told you 'bout that, boy?' he continued. 'Has she told you she murdered a US marshal?' Jonathan glanced very nervously at his sister and licked his lips. 'She said they don't like it when one of their own gets murdered an' she's right about that,' continued Brogan. 'They'll be lookin' for her. I'd have nothin' to do with it if I was you.'

'Nice try, Mr McNally,' she said, laughing and raising her rifle. 'OK, so you might fool one or two by takin' his body back, but you're still wanted for the murder of my pa and brothers. Nobody is going to believe you.'

'You do though, don't you, boy?' Brogan said to Jonathan. 'You know as well as I do what I'm sayin' is the truth.' Once again Jonathan looked very nervous and shuffled uneasily. 'That's right, Jonathan,' continued Brogan. 'I'd feel mighty uneasy in your situation too. I'd be thinkin': maybe I'm next.'

'It won't do you any good trying to

set him against me,' said Betty. 'We've come to an arrangement. He gets the ranch because he's entitled to it then he sells out to me just as he is legally entitled to do. He gets the money he wants, I get the land I want. A perfect solution for both of us.'

'Perfect!' said Brogan with a wry smile. 'If you believe that, Jonathan, then you're not half as bright as I thought you were. I don't know if she told you she'd killed the marshal, but it's the truth. She probably didn't, I can see by the look on your face she didn't. Did she also tell you what she did to them two men she hired to kill you?' Betty looked slightly alarmed. 'Well, she didn't actually do a damned thing herself. She had two of your Indian friends practise a few old, traditional tortures on 'em. I found 'em back there tied between trees, their eyes torn out an' their bodies almost slashed to pieces. One of 'em was still alive though. He lived long enough to tell me that she said it was payment for them *not* killin' you. I reckon she might be plannin' somethin' like that for you an' possibly even me.'

Jonathan looked at his sister and licked his lips again.

'What's he talkin' about?' he asked her. 'You told me all these two were doing was looking for me to bring me back.'

'They were,' hissed Betty. 'Don't listen to him.'

'That's right, Jonathan,' said Brogan. 'Don't listen to a dirty old saddle tramp like me. I mean, I did kill your pa an' brothers didn't I? At least that's what you'd like the law to think.'

Betty Crossland suddenly raised her rifle and aimed at Brogan but Brogan knew enough of human nature to know that she was not going to squeeze the trigger just yet. She had to say her piece.

'I ought to kill you right here an' now,' she hissed. 'I might just do that anyway. I would be more than justified, everybody believes you murdered my father and brothers. Revenge killings are always looked upon very kindly.'

'Does everybody believe I did it?' goaded Brogan. 'I wouldn't be too sure about that if I was you, Miss Betty. Before he died, the marshal told me that he'd had a visit from Luke Briscoe, the farrier from Driftwood. Seems like there was another witness to what really happened.'

'Impossible!' snapped Betty. 'I made certain there was nobody else about. You're bluffing, Mr McNally. He never mentioned this to Jonathan.'

'Am I?' said Brogan. 'It's a pity you can't ask the marshal himself. He never mentioned it because the witness didn't see Jonathan kill his pa, he or she only saw *you* kill your brothers. He was hopin' Jonathan would persuade you to go back to Sulphur Springs with him. Now, if you don't mind, Miss Betty, I've got a long way to go. I'll bid you a good day.' He urged his horse forward. 'I wouldn't let her get behind me if I was you, boy.'

228

'Are you just goin' to let him ride out of here?' Jonathan suddenly screamed at his sister. 'He'll get us both hanged.'

'I guess he's right,' said Betty. 'This is as far as you go, McNally. I'll take my chances with the law.'

Brogan turned slightly in his saddle, a single shot roared out and Betty Crossland screamed as the rifle spun out of her hands. She gazed in horror at her now shattered hand. Jonathan stared in disbelief and dropped his rifle.

'You'd best get that seen to as soon as possible,' said Brogan. 'Things like that have a habit of goin' bad ways out here. I could've killed you easy enough, Miss Betty, I could kill you both right now, but I ain't in the habit of killin' women or children. I wouldn't bother to follow me an' try to sneak up on me either. I'll know exactly where you are long before you'll know where I am. Oh, an' don't rely on your Indian friends either. They might be good but I'm better. See you in Sulphur Springs sometime.'

10

Despite Brogan's warning to Betty and Jonathan Crossland that he was a better bushman and tracker than the Indian policemen, he knew full well that good as he was it was something of an empty boast. He was fully aware that a good Indian tracker would be more than a match for him.

He continued his journey for most of the remaining couple of daylight hours, making camp shortly before sunset, when he came across a large, deep pool of clear water, just off the main trail. He decided to light a fire, knowing that not to do so would make very little difference to the Indians who, if they were following him, would know exactly where he was.

As he had travelled he had kept a constant watch and a keen ear for any signs of them but had not detected any.

However, in such circumstances, he always assumed the worst possible scenario and was quite prepared to believe that they were not that far behind.

The choice of the pool of water was not made simply because it had been the only source of good, clean water available for some time, but because its depth and size afforded him some form of protection. With the deep pool on one side, a sixty-foot sheer cliff-face rising from the water and sweeping round to form an overhang, still part of the cliff, on another side, which would give protection from any attack from above, it meant that he had only one direction to really worry about and that was easily defended.

There were plenty of fish in the water, some of them quite large and Brogan even attempted to catch one which came within reach, but failed dismally.

Since water and Brogan McNally had never been the best of friends, he had generally fought shy of trying to catch fish if only for no other reason that doing so inevitably involved his getting wet. He *had* managed to catch fish on the odd occasion, but his success had almost always been down to pure luck rather than judgement and had always been in shallow rivers or streams, never deep pools. He had never been particularly fond of the taste of fish in any case, something that probably had more to do with his lack of skill in catching them than the actual taste. Generally speaking though, he ate to survive, not for enjoyment.

In this particular instance, the water appeared to be at least ten feet deep even close to the edge and further out the bottom could not be seen. Because of his dislike of water in general and mistrust of deep or fast-flowing water in particular, he had never learnt the art of swimming. It was one of the very few skills he did not possess and one which he had on occasion regretted not acquiring. However it was an oversight he most certainly had no intention of correcting at such a late stage of his life.

As far as he was concerned water, essential as it might be in many ways, was strictly for drinking and cooking. Its deliberate application to the skin was not to be encouraged and, even when it might be deemed necessary so to do for cleansing purposes, must only be applied very sparingly. Normally it was only applied to face or hands and then only when *absolutely* essential. Even so he had, on occasion, been known to splash water on his neck and face or even immerse his head in order to cool himself down in exceptionally hot or dusty conditions, but he did not count that as *washing*.

Total voluntary immersion happened to him only in rare instances, usually when being forced to cross deep rivers but, in his opinion, it was otherwise unnatural, especially when heated, mixed with soap and deliberately applied.

On the few occasions he had been

subjected to soap and hot water — always when he was completely powerless to prevent such a disaster and always carried out by otherwise apparently well-intentioned women — as far as he was concerned he had been proved right. He had caught a cold each time it had happened which was more than ample evidence to him that it *was* totally unnatural. He claimed that soap and hot water took essential protective oils out of the body.

However, he was still hungry and there were no more beans or salt pork. He eventually solved his hunger problem when he accidentally encountered a large rattlesnake. Things like rattlesnakes he could deal with without thinking. He quickly and expertly killed the snake and soon had it cooking over the fire. He looked about for edible roots or tubers but could not find any.

'Heard you talkin' to the Crossland woman,' Marshal Simpson suddenly and most unexpectedly croaked as Brogan placed his billy on the fire to make some coffee. 'At least you're definitely in the clear for the murders.'

'So you say,' said Brogan, 'but I want to hear it from a judge or somebody else in authority. For that to happen I have to get you back to Sulphur Springs an' a doctor.'

'You're probably right,' admitted the marshal. 'Do I smell coffee?'

'Just brewin',' replied Brogan. 'You been awake long?'

'Most of the time we've been on the move,' said the marshal. 'Even I find it difficult to sleep when I'm being bounced all over the place. Nice touch that, pretending I was dead.'

'You didn't say nothin',' said Brogan.

'No point,' replied the marshal. 'You had other things on your mind, such as the Indians.'

'You heard me say that they'd caught an' tortured Bremner an' Tex?' asked Brogan. 'I didn't think you were awake when I found 'em. It wasn't a pretty sight. I've seen an' heard of some things in all the years I've been driftin' but I

235

ain't seen nothin' like that since I was a boy. In them days some Indians had never even seen a white man an' I think they were more scared of us than we was of them. I reckon what them Indians did was definitely against the law though.'

'I heard,' confirmed the marshal. 'I know them two shouldn't've been on the reservation but that don't mean the Indians can just kill 'em when an' how they've a mind to. I'll have them arrested when we get back.'

'At least you said *when* an' not *if*,' said Brogan. 'Only thing is, I seem to remember you more or less givin' them permission to do just what the hell they wanted to.'

'They know just how far they can go,' grunted the marshal.

'OK, maybe I got it wrong,' conceded Brogan with more than a hint of sarcasm. 'I can't help thinkin' though that them Indians might not be too happy for me to reach Sulphur Springs an' tell what I saw, even if they do think you're dead. I have this feelin' they're goin' to be trouble an' I never ignore my feelin's. That's why I've survived so long.'

'I don't know much about you, McNally,' said the marshal, 'but I've seen and heard enough to know that if anybody can deal with them, you can.'

'I sure hope so,' said Brogan. 'I ain't gettin' no younger though. Lately I find it harder to wake up in the mornin'. Are you hungry? I got me some rattlesnake roastin' if you fancy a piece.'

'Naw,' croaked the marshal. 'Right now I don't think any food would stay down. I've had rattlesnake a few times so I know it tastes fine. I would appreciate a coffee though. My throat's as dry as the Black Rock Desert an' the last rain there was more'n two years ago.'

'Comin' right up' said Brogan. 'You just hang on in there until we get back to Sulphur Springs, Marshal, you're the only proof I've got I didn't kill the Crosslands. By the way, talkin' about rattlesnakes, just before he died, Greasy Bremner said somethin' about the Indians meetin' up with Betty Crossland at some place called Rattlesnake Rocks. Where's that?'

'That was where you met up with the Crosslands,' said the marshal.

'Thought it might be,' said Brogan. 'Don't know where they was but I guess the Indians know for sure where we are now. I guess we'll just have to wait an' see what happens.'

Brogan was not too surprised when the night passed uneventfully. He had listened for sounds which would indicate the presence of the Indians but he had not heard any. In fact he had been rather more concerned by the presence of a mountain lion coming to drink and which showed rather too much interest in the horses which in turn had been very restless. However, the big cat had been very wary about the presence of Brogan and the marshal. To Brogan's and the horses' relief the animal had eventually retreated.

If the Indians knew where he was they were obviously wise enough not to try and attack somewhere where they could easily get themselves killed. They would wait for more open or better ambush country and Brogan knew there would be plenty of both between the pool and Sulphur Springs.

★ ★ ★

It was about midday when Brogan suddenly pulled both horses between two large rocks and amongst some dense brush. The marshal was awake and looked up questioningly. Brogan dismounted, took his rifle and placed a finger against his lips to tell the marshal to remain quiet. He ventured forward on foot using all available cover to hide his presence.

Brogan was not at all certain as to why he had stopped. Even he was uncertain whether it had been something he had heard or simply sensed. Whatever it was he chose not to ignore it and eventually, as he crawled under some bushes, he was looking down into a very narrow gully into which the trail disappeared.

There was no obvious way of avoiding the gully, at least not with a horse. The land either side was mainly bare rock with a few stunted bushes and clumps of coarse grass growing between gaps in the rock. Narrow ledges, no more than two or three feet wide, ran along the top of the gully and about fifteen feet above the trail. From there the rock face rose almost sheer and perfectly smoothly to a height of about sixty feet on the left side of the gully to where there seemed to be another but wider ledge. It then rose almost at least another 200 or even 300 feet. On the right side of the gully there was no second ledge, it simply rose sheer for at least 300 feet. It was obvious that it would have been impossible to take the horses along either of the lower ledges.

Quite apart from getting up to the

higher ledge appearing to be impossible, it seemed to disappear completely after about 400 yards. The ones on either side of the top of the gully were probably quite easy to reach but they were far too narrow and with too many rocks to allow horses or the marshal's litter to pass freely. The only other way of avoiding the gully appeared to be to return the way he had come and choose a different direction.

He studied the gully for some considerable length of time and in all that time his senses still told him that all was not as it appeared. Eventually his feelings were vindicated when he detected a movement amongst some rocks above the entrance to the gully.

At first it was very slight, but it had been enough to convince Brogan that somebody *was* waiting in ambush. This was confirmed when the figure of a uniformed Indian suddenly appeared from behind a rock some sixty or seventy feet above the gully. He had obviously been keeping watch for Brogan.

He descended into the gully and disappeared. Whether it had been this man who had in some way alerted Brogan he neither knew nor cared but he was reasonably certain that the Indian had not seen him.

Brogan returned to the marshal and explained what he was up against. The marshal suggested that they return and find another way through but that would add at least two days to their journey. Although the marshal appeared to be a little better, he was still very critical and Brogan was not prepared to risk another two days. That apart, as ever, his stubborn streak refused to be beaten.

'I'm goin' to leave you here,' he told the marshal. 'I'll leave you with a gun and some bullets just in case they find you. There's plenty of cover so they probably won't and I'll obliterate the tracks leadin' here just to make sure. What you do with the gun is up to you if they do happen to find you. Mind, I have me this feelin' that they just might make certain you *are* dead this time if they do. I'm goin' to try an' get along the top of the gully. They won't be expectin' somethin' like that an' I can probably pick them off.'

'Or they will pick *you* off,' said the marshal.

'Or they'll pick me off,' agreed Brogan. 'If that happens I guess what becomes of you won't be no interest to me no more. There might only be the two of 'em or Betty an' Jonathan Crossland could be with 'em,' Brogan continued. 'Thing is, if somebody tries to shoot me I'll probably shoot first an' worry who it was later. I just might kill the Crosslands. I want them alive if possible an' I guess you do too. Just thought I'd better warn you, though.'

'Point taken, McNally.' The marshal grinned. 'I've heard enough to know you didn't murder the other Crosslands an' I can assure you my word is good enough. You just make sure you don't get yourself killed. If you die I reckon I do too. Now get goin' an' don't take too long. I think there's a rattler here somewhere. I heard it just now. It'd be a pity if I was to die of a snake-bite after all this.'

'You just keep still an' it probably won't bother you,' said Brogan. 'They normally only strike to kill for food or if they're scared. They get well out of the way if they possibly can. I slept with one under my blanket all night once an' he never bit me.'

'Yeah,' grinned the marshal, 'that was probably 'cos you smell so bad he thought you were a dung heap an' they like dung heaps.'

Brogan grunted something obscene and disappeared.

★ ★ ★

Having made certain that there was no look-out, Brogan was just about to climb up on to the left ledge above the gully — this one being the easiest to reach and appearing to offer the best cover — when he was suddenly forced to dive between two large rocks. Two horses galloped out of the gully, the riders quite plainly being the Indian policemen. They raced off back along the trail.

Brogan had been taken by surprise but he was not slow to recover his composure. It had been his intention to travel along the gully since it was the only way through and he realized that it was a case of now or never. He too raced back to where he had left the marshal.

'Let's get out of here,' he gasped. 'Them two Indians went harin' off for some reason I don't know about. We might be able to get through before they come back. Even if they do come back that gully is narrow enough to defend an' they'll know that. They'll wait until we're in more open country.'

'You're runnin' this show,' grunted the marshal. 'Is there anythin' particular you want me to do?'

'Just pull that blanket over your head an' keep on playin' dead,' said Brogan.

'It could be that Betty an' Jonathan Crossland are there an' I want them to carry on thinkin' you're dead. I reckon them an' the Indians came past us durin' the night. Miss Betty and Jonathan I can deal with blindfold. Right, hang on, let's go, it's goin' to be a fast an' bumpy ride.'

'You mean it hasn't been bumpy already?' grunted the marshal.

Even Brogan's old horse appeared to sense the urgency and seemed quite willing to move rather faster than normal. They entered the gully with Brogan holding his rifle at the ready and his keen eyes on the alert for the slightest sign of danger.

They had travelled about 300 yards when the figures of Betty Crossland and her brother, both with rifles, stepped into view at a slightly wider part of the gully. They were about fifty yards away from Brogan. He stopped quickly, knowing that although he was within range of their rifles, it would still take a good shot to cause him any real injury. He, on the other hand, was quite confident of being able to kill them both at that distance if necessary.

'I seen your friends hightail it outa here,' called Brogan. 'What they done, run out on you?'

'Very clever, Mr McNally,' called Betty. 'Fortunately for you they don't appreciate your abilities like I do. They wouldn't listen to me. They don't seem to be able to understand that any white man can possibly know enough to outwit them. Just goes to show that men are the same all the world over. Indian men are just like most white men, so full of themselves. They think they know everything while us poor womenfolk don't know a damned thing. They'll be back though. They couldn't understand why you hadn't reached here before now. They know you spent the night alongside that pool of water.'

'Guessed they might've done,' said Brogan. 'How's the hand, Miss Betty?' he asked. 'Even with a shattered hand you still have the advantage. There's two of you an' you probably think you can kill me between you.'

'Possibly we could, Mr McNally,' she agreed. 'However, I am not stupid enough to tempt fate. I know that you are most certainly a better shot than me even if you hadn't shot my hand to pieces. I'm a pretty damned good shot even if I say so myself, but now I have no chance. You are most certainly a better shot than Jonathan will ever be. Not only that, you seem to have this unfortunate knack of surviving so I'm not stupid enough to believe I can outwit you. You can pass through if you want to, I won't stop you.'

'Very wise of you,' said Brogan.

'Not wise, Mr McNally,' she said, 'just practical. This is Indian country, they know it, you don't. You won't get far.'

'Like you said, Miss Betty,' said Brogan, 'I have this knack of survival. It might be unfortunate as far as you are concerned but I think I'm very fortunate, although it's less down to

248

good fortune an' a whole lot more to do with a great number of years of experience. I've been around a long time now, too long sometimes I think. I'm not ready to die just yet though. OK, I'm comin' through but I'd feel a mite safer if you weren't behind me with them guns.'

She laughed loudly.

'Then I guess you'll just have to stay where you are and wait for the Indians to return. They intend to kill you, Mr McNally, they know you've seen what they did to Greasy Bremner and his friend and they know they are likely to hang for that if anyone ever finds out. They just want to make sure you never live to tell anyone.'

'And what about you two, Miss Betty?' asked Brogan. 'You know what they did as well. In fact I know you encouraged them. Greasy Bremner wasn't dead when I found 'em. He lived long enough to tell me what happened. But then I've told you all this already.'

'I had nothing to do with it and you'll

never be able to prove I did,' she replied.

'My point is,' continued Brogan. 'You know what they did. They might not want to take the chance that you wouldn't say nothin'. I reckon they'll kill you as well just as soon as they think they need to. Are you hearin' what I'm sayin', boy?' he said to Jonathan who until that point had said nothing. 'I don't know if you saw what they did, but it wasn't a pretty sight. They gouged out their eyes. I'd hate to think they might just do the same thing to you.'

'Sorry, Mr McNally, I'll take that chance,' said Jonathan. 'Betty's right about neither of us not tryin' to stop you now but we won't be far behind.'

'Then I suppose I'd better get goin',' said Brogan. 'Hold your nose when the marshal goes past, he's beginnin' to smell a bit. In fact we've had us a buzzard followin' us most of the way. Damned stupid bird seemed to think I was carryin' his dinner.'

He laughed loudly at his supposed joke and urged his and the marshal's horse forward. At the same time he kept a wary eye on both Betty and Jonathan. Although Jonathan fingered his rifle in anticipation, he noted that Betty laid a restraining hand on his arm. He turned and raised his tattered hat in sarcastic acknowledgement to them before disappearing.

* * *

Brogan made good time through the gully, which proved to be longer than he had expected. It suddenly opened up into one side of a broad and fairly flat-bottomed valley through which a wide but shallow-looking river meandered. The valley floor was strewn with rounded, water-worn rocks making any crossing quite difficult. There were plenty of lush bushes and shrubs but hardly any trees of any size. There appeared to be two possible routes.

'Which way?' he asked the marshal.

'There looks to be two valleys up ahead both goin' in the general direction of Sulphur Springs.'

'I can't rightly see,' said the marshal, 'but I'd guess we've reached the Jackson River. Just keep on followin' the main river upstream through the left hand of the two valleys. After about five miles there's a set of rapids and a waterfall. At the top of the falls head east for another five miles or so until you find yourself at the top of a high cliff overlooking Sulphur Springs. You can't miss it. The cliff is maybe six hundred feet high. It could be a bit tricky gettin' down but there are one or two ways. If you can't get down it means a detour of about another half-day.'

'In the meantime I think we got us some company,' said Brogan. 'They've been followin' us from about half-way through the gully. I don't think it's just the Crosslands either.'

'I suppose it was only a matter of time,' grunted the marshal. 'Reckon you can handle them? I probably won't be much use.'

'I've survived worse,' said Brogan. 'If it's about five miles to these falls, an' if it's a place that can be defended I think that'd be the best place to stop for the night. You know it, is it a good place?'

'You should be able to hold them off,' confirmed the marshal. 'The only problem is it'll be easy for them to get ahead of us.'

'That's somethin' we'll have to face when we come to it,' said Brogan. 'Now you just keep that blanket pulled over your head an' quit talkin'. You're supposed to be dead, remember.'

For about the first two miles to the falls the road was narrow, followed the slightly higher ground at the edge of the river-bed, and there were very few places where anyone could have passed them unseen. Long before then though, Brogan had pin-pointed the exact position of his pursuers and it appeared that they were making little effort to keep their presence secret. But then they had no need.

Actually Brogan was quite pleased with this. To him it meant that they were becoming rather too confident and, in his experience, that was almost always a failing as it usually led to carelessness.

After about two miles the land started to rise, became covered in large boulders and, although plainly much more difficult than the road they were on, there were obviously a great many ways for anyone to get ahead. Most of them appeared to involve steep, narrow tracks between the boulders, all of which looked too difficult to drag a litter along. It was shortly after entering this terrain that Brogan sensed that his pursuers were no longer behind him.

He had not seen or even heard them, but he now knew that the danger was from the front and not behind. The falls were reached with no further problems and Brogan chose a sheltered spot overlooking most of the surrounding land. Once again he lit a fire.

'Seems like they've got in front of us,' he said to the marshal. 'I don't reckon there'll be any trouble tonight but I reckon that if they are goin' to make a move they can't leave it much longer. I reckon it'll be in the mornin'.'

'Still want me to play dead?' asked the marshal. 'I've still got my gun and I've been thinking. I might be of some use.'

'If they know you're alive you'll be their first target,' assured Brogan. 'With you out of the way, even if I somehow manage to survive, it'll be my word against theirs as to what happened both with the Crosslands an' with Greasy Bremner. If that is the case I know darned well who will be believed. No, Marshal, you stay alive an' don't attract no trouble.'

★ ★ ★

As expected, the night passed without any trouble and when they started out just after dawn there was no sign of anyone. Brogan's senses also told him that he was not in any immediate danger, but he still maintained his vigilance. However, even he was more than surprised when they reached the cliff overlooking Sulphur Springs without any problems.

There were a couple of ways down the cliff face and had he been alone Brogan would have had no problems in negotiating the 600- or 700-foot descent, but taking the litter down that way was plainly out of the question.

'Which way?' he muttered, pulling alongside the marshal who was still pretending to be dead. 'Ain't no way I'm goin' to get you down that way. We'll both end up goin' over the edge. Don't move, you're dead, remember.'

'East,' whispered the marshal. 'Four or five hours. There's a steep pass between two peaks. You can't miss it, it's the only way wagons can get up or down an' the way most folk use. You probably came up that way when you left Sulphur Springs.'

'I remember it,' said Brogan.

Suddenly he sat up straight in his saddle, drew his rifle from the saddle holster and held it hip-high, ready to shoot. Then he turned his horse so that his back was towards the cliff and looked down.

'I'd say we got company,' he whispered. 'Can't see nor hear nobody but I knows they're there all right. I was wonderin' what had happened to 'em. Keep on playin' dead, Marshal. Just leave everythin' to me.' He slipped the rifle back in the holster. 'I'm goin' to act like I know nothin',' he continued. 'OK, I'll head east. Maybe they won't try nothin' just here, it's a bit too open.'

Brogan led the marshal's horse away from the edge of the cliff and along a fairly well-marked trail. After about half a mile the trail narrowed as it entered a short but steep-sided cutting. It was too narrow and short to be called a valley but too wide to be a gully. There were no obvious places, apart from one, for anyone to hide or ambush him and he could see the end of the cutting less than half a mile away. Nevertheless his senses were screaming *danger* at him. However, there was no way of avoiding the cutting.

Quite suddenly, shortly after he had entered the cutting, there was the sound of horses behind him. At the same time two figures appeared from behind the only large rock in the cutting about thirty yards in front of him. These two were quite plainly Betty and Jonathan Crossland. He looked back and saw the two Indian policemen closing in on him, their horses now pulled up to a walking pace.

'Looks like you got me trapped,' he called out to the Crosslands. 'I must be gettin' old, I don't normally allow myself to be boxed in so easy.'

'It was just a matter of time, Mr McNally,' called Betty Crossland. 'You might be very good, but even you couldn't outwit them for ever, dumb though they might be. They listened to what I had to say this time and it worked. Now there are two guns in front of you and two behind and I don't think even you can shoot in both directions at once. I've been practising and I think I can use this gun well enough to kill you should I need to. However, I don't think I shall have to. I am quite certain my two friends will do all that is necessary. They had some idea about you going through what Bremner did.'

Brogan looked back and saw that the two Indians had dismounted about fifty yards behind and were slowly advancing. Betty and Jonathan Crossland held their ground. Brogan nodded and laughed drily.

'Looks like I made a serious miscalculation about you, Miss Betty,' he called. 'I ain't afraid of dyin', it's got to happen to us all sometime.' The Indian policemen were now only about twenty feet away and once again Brogan laughed drily. 'I reckon you're close enough so's I can take at least one of you with me,' he said to them. 'Which one is it to be? I don't much care.'

This appeared to make both men stop and apparently think. They fingered their rifles a little nervously. Quite suddenly gunfire echoed around the sides of the cutting.

Exactly how many shots there had been Brogan was not at all certain. The only thing of which he was certain was that none of them had been fired by him. Both Indians stared in apparent disbelief for a few moments before allowing their rifles to slip from their grasp as they too slowly sank to the ground.

'Do you believe in miracles, Miss Betty?' Brogan called. 'I guess I just witnessed one. Seems like the marshal has rose from the dead an' just shot your two friends.'

Her answer was to fire her rifle rather wildly in Brogan's direction but the shot was well wide. Suddenly both she and her brother were running. Their horses were hidden behind the boulder. Brogan laughed but made no attempt to follow. He looked down on the marshal.

'It hurt like hell an' nearly killed me but I said I might be of some use, didn't I?' said the marshal.

'I was relyin' on it,' replied Brogan with a broad smile.

★　★　★

A day later Doc Heidelmann pronounced that Marshal James Simpson would make a full recovery. Judge Liam Storey confirmed that Brogan was no longer wanted for any murders and that he was free to go.

Sheriff Michael Seaton, acting for the marshal, organized a posse to track down Betty Crossland and her brother and Brogan remained in Sulphur Springs just long enough to see them both arrested.

'Just goes to show things ain't always what they seem,' Brogan said to her. 'You had your chances to kill me, you should've taken them. Most folk seem to make that mistake.'

'You're not human!' she snarled. 'You are nothin' but an animal.'

'Animals don't kill for pleasure, Miss Betty,' he said. 'Maybe we could all learn a thing or two from them. Anyhow, if they don't hang you, I reckon you an' Jonathan will have a good many years to think about it. I wouldn't bother thinkin' about revenge on me either. I'll be long gone from this earth when you get out, if you ever do.'

'And I hope you rot in hell!' she rasped.

'At least it'll be warm down there,' Brogan said with a wry laugh. 'One thing I hate more'n anythin' else is the cold. Cold an' snow. Ain't no chance of either in hell so they tell me.'

WEST OF EDEN

Mike Stall

Marshal Jack Adams was tired of people shooting at him. So when the kid came into town sporting a two-gun rig and out to make his reputation — at Adams' expense — it was time to turn in his star and buy that horse ranch he'd dreamed about in the Eden Valley. It looked peaceful, but the valley was on the verge of a range-war and there was only one man to stop it. So Adams pinned on a star again and started shooting back — with a vengeance!

BAR 10 GUNSMOKE

Boyd Cassidy

As always, Bar 10 rancher Gene Adams responded to a plea for help, taking Johnny Puma and Tomahawk. They headed into Mexico to help their friend Don Miguel Garcia. But they were walking into a trap laid by the outlaw known as Lucifer. When the Bar 10 riders arrived at Garcia's ranch, Johnny was cut down in a hail of bullets. Adams and Tomahawk thunder into action to take on Lucifer and his gang. But will they survive the outlaws' hot lead?

THE FRONTIERSMEN

Elliot Conway

Major Philip Gaunt and his former batman, Naik Alif Khan, veterans of dozens of skirmishes on British India's north-west frontier, are fighting the wild and dangerous land of northern Mexico. Aided by 'Buckskin' Carlson, a newly reformed drunk, they are hunting down Mexican bandidos who murdered the major's sister. But it proves to be a dangerous trail. Death by knife and gun is never far away. Will they finally deliver cold justice to the bandidos?